UNACCOMPANIED MINORS

[STORIES]

Also by Alden Jones

The Blind Masseuse:
A Traveler's Memoir from Costa Rica to Cambodia

UNACCOMPANIED MINORS

[STORIES]

BY

ALDEN JONES

new american press

Milwaukee, Wis. • Urbana, Ill.

new american press

www.NewAmericanPress.com

Printed in the United States of America
ISBN 978-0-9849439-9-9
Cover design by David Bowen
Cover photo of Esther Gutow by Alden Jones
Interior layout by Nicole Weber

Some of these stories appeared previously in the following journals: "Shelter" in the *Barcelona Review*; "Something Will Grow" in *Prairie Schooner* and in an earlier version in *Washington Square*; "Heathens" in *AGNI*; and "Sin Alley" in *Midway Journal.*

For ordering information, please contact:
Ingram Book Group
One Ingram Blvd.
La Vergne, TN 37086
(800) 937-8000
orders@ingrambook.com

TABLE OF CONTENTS

SHELTER

We're in a homeless shelter in Asheville, NC. We think it's funny. How did all these people in some hellish hickish place like Asheville, NC, get homeless, that's what we want to know. It's so crowded we have to sleep on the floor.

I'm with this dyke Spike who I met in Ft Lauderdale, FL. She's got an old white Toyota and a tent where we've been sleeping the past month. She wanted to see the Appalachians so there we were, trekking up stony trails and putting four drops of iodine in each bottle of slimy river water, sleeping in the bags she lifted from her roommate's brother out of the garage. We took his stove, too, and a flashlight, he's probably hot on our trail looking for Spike so he can pulp her little body with his big faggy boots. Problem is his stuff was meant for the Everglades, that's what Spike says, where it's hot, and now it's October, last night we drank four cups each of hot cocoa and wound up leaving the tent all night to take one piss after another, Appalachian trail air biting our asses. I say Fuck this and we start fingering our options and Spike says, I wonder if there's a homeless shelter around here, and I say that would be fun, let's see who's in there all hard up, so we drive down the mountain to the highway and find a Waffle House with a phone book, and count fifteen fast-food restaurants on our way here.

Spike helps my image because I'm all woman whereas Spike looks like a fourteen-year-old boy all limbs and sinew. The first thing she sees at the shelter is the basketball net out on the blacktop and the next thing I know she's out shooting baskets with some pocked-up Mexican guys and I want to know, how in the hell did these Mexican guys make it all the way to Asheville, NC, just to wind up homeless. But Spike likes making friends which is ok by me as long as she'll toss them off later and come back to me, which she does. Usually by nine o'clock she's slammed and I can make her say anything I want her to say because Spike always wants to get back in my pants. I made the mistake once or twice of being too drunk to care if she shimmied my jeans down my legs, so she's done that, back in Ft. Lauderdale when she lived over Chaussie's where a bottle of Miller was eighty-five cents. I never felt a thing, but Spike thinks it means I'm a dyke like her and keeps waiting for my next blackout, blackouts being something like a sign of true love for Spike, which is kind of sad.

So Spike's out with the guys, practicing her Spanish saying cabrón and maricón and asking them to teach her new "cuss words," as words like shit and fuck and faggot are known to be called in this place, the South. I go into the shelter and look all destitute for the bleached-out woman running the show, which to be honest wasn't hard after all those nights fighting no-see-ums and rolling around in the dirt of Grandfather Mountain. Spike was always trying to roll over on me even while she slept, so sometimes I did, actually, sleep in the dirt outside, just to get a decent night's sleep. The woman, all pouty, takes pity on me, and gives me towels and blankets, and I start roaming around the place. It looks like my elementary school. There's a library, a cafeteria, a big scary kitchen and then a few rooms with cots where the desks would have been.

Spike comes in all energized smelling salty like sweat and we decide to lie down, test the floor. It's covered in a blue-speckled carpet but still, truly harder than the slab of mountain known as Grandfather. Poor Spike on her bony butt already feels cagey to get on her feet, so she gets up, does that little dance she does to shake off her energy, and pulls me up and leads me outside. See, I'm a very lazy person by nature and Spike is good for me this way, always making me do things. My womanly body is quite cushy enough to make the floor a comfortable place for a while. But that's not productive, now is it.

The Mexican guys are gone so we sit down on the porch and Spike rolls up a Drum. She says she smokes Drum because it has no impurities but I know she likes to roll her own tobacco so she can feel more like a cowboy. I start calling her Cowboy then, poking her with my toe, and she gets all cute and shy-acting and starts throwing bits of tobacco at me which look just like the freeze-dried blood worms we used to feed to her Japanese fighting fish back in Ft. Lauderdale, FL, the same fish that is probably rotting away on the top of the fish bowl about now. Poor Sticky.

A girl comes out and we shut up so we can find out her story. Her name's Jamie. She's fat like bad fruit and has a head full of bleach. A bad perm. Too much sperm, actually, Jamie's eight months pregnant. She tells us this is her third and she's given the other two away but this one she's keeping. Too bad the father's married and wants nothing to do with her or her offspring. We ask her why didn't she just have an abortion and Jamie says she doesn't believe in it, which really pisses Spike off. See, Spike has this thing for girls who are content to be stomped on by men: she hates them. Now if Jamie would cry or bitch and moan about how-could-he-do-this-to-me, Spike would give her a speech about how her life could be better, that is how to be more like Spike herself, a dyke that is, and make friends with her—but the girl's all smug and satisfied, dragging on her Kool. Clearly this dear Jamie is straighter than Spike can fathom, even Spike doesn't want this convert. Then Jamie tells us the shelter has found her an apartment and is even paying for it. She's moving in tomorrow. Now, this really pisses us off because why don't they pay for us to have a place, since I'm smart enough to buy condoms and Spike's smart enough to be a dyke and neither of us are stupid enough to have three babies by the time we're twenty, now why don't we get rewarded for that? But Jamie's too soft to deal with that kind of philosophizing, no she's no match for truth, so she puts out her menthol and goes back inside all teary and worldweary like she's Atlas and we're just poking at her ribs for no good reason. Spike and I decide that most homeless people must try to blame everyone else for their problems all the time, and just as we decide this we meet JT. JT's a black guy from East Orange, NJ, and he's wearing pantyhose on his head and proving our point. "Drugs," he tells us, he rounds it out like a belch, like the word is finite and begins and ends all at once and tells the whole story. I ask him why he came all the way down to Asheville, NC, just to be on drugs. He tells us that's the point, he came sticksbound on the run from drugs, but even in Asheville, NC, your little friends find you. Spike and I find this really dull and tell him why doesn't he just drink like a normal law-abiding person and save himself the travel expenses. We say Actually, we're going up through that place known as the Garden State and why doesn't he join us and we'll get him trashed every night and he can see how easy it is to be off drugs and he can get home free. JT laughs but then stares real hard at Spike like he's just figuring out she's a dyke. He gives that crooked old suspicious look, just like any hick would. We think maybe he belongs down here.

We're quite a team, me and Spike. People can't figure out what the hell we are, we're like Jack Sprat (that would be Spike) and Jack Sprat's wife (that would be me), but we're both girls, so they don't know how to treat us. Spiffy and sweet, all male authority as if it were just me alone? I have a good giggle and I like to play with my long red locks when strangers talk to me. Or boy-buddy elbowing as if it were just Spike. She likes a good jostle. So we raid the kitchen and nobody stops us because we're just too fast for them to pin us down. It's fun, we fill scraped-up green plastic cups from the thousand-gallon iced tea dispenser and I find a whole bushel of bananas, and we're peeling them one by one and throwing them on the floor, having the time of our lives until I discover a huge shaker of MSG on the shelf—"Flavor Enhancer" it says—and get grossed out. We consider a ploy to wipe out the homeless population in Asheville, NC, by MSG poisoning and wonder what that means in terms of the contents of the iced tea. We dump it out in the sink that's big enough for Spike to bathe in. A shame since we're all dry with thirst. We haven't had anything real to drink since last night when I pocketed a fifth of Jack Daniels while Spike distracted the guy by buying four cans of Strohs. See, that's why Spike needs me, because I'm so sweet no one would think to accuse me of lifting. But now we're dry. No booze inside, they told us on the phone, no drugs and no alcohol and no sexual relations and Spike and I got a good laugh out of that, knowing we could NEVER be homeless if those were the rules. Especially Spike who has to sleep in a room full of girls. They checked us all out before they gave us our towels and blankets and we knew enough to have nothing on us that they could dump out and waste.

But now we're empty and itching from this, and Spike gets all jumpy and bugged when this happens and we have to find something to keep us entertained. We go out to the rec room where this skinny black guy is playing chess by himself. He's simmering all pleasant and notices us but doesn't get distracted, just looks at us once and then back to his blacks and whites, kings and queens and all those sorry little pawns. I'm watching him and Spike's jostling the chair we're sharing and beginning to get on my nerves. I start thinking this guy is like God, like God who kills who he wants but sometimes gets tangled up in destinies even God doesn't realize he's creating, and suddenly the piece you least expect is in the perfect square to get crushed and that sense of creating what you least expected must be the only thing that keeps God from getting bored, playing by himself all the time. But then Spike interrupts this thought which is threading around my brain so pleasantly and says Let's get out of this soulsucking place and hit the road. I smack the top of Spike's puny little head and tell her to shut up and stop ruining my night. All right, says Spike, as soon as you get your tight ass to unclench you violent priss. I cross my arms and try to look seriously annoyed for Spike, but she doesn't do what I expect her to do, which is say Angel—that's my name—don't be mad, cut it out Angel, with that femme-y pleading look she usually saves for me. Instead she shuts up all right. It's rare for Spike to shut up so I don't know what to do next. I'm still waiting for her to come around when she gets up and goes over to the table, sits down with the guy, and grabs a rook and slides it across a few squares.

I think she's going to get it for screwing up this guy's game and I'm all set to take her hand and run her out of there, but the guy rubs his chin and lets out a big Hmmmm, and moves a knight into the middle of the board. Spike taps her fingers on the table until I think I might explode. Where did Spike learn to play chess, that's what I want to know. Her little hand hovers over a pawn until I can't stand it anymore. I lunge toward the chess board and grab Spike's queen because if there's one thing I know about this game it's that the queen is the piece that really matters, she's always the one looking out for the king while the king moves one lazyass square at a time, and you know you're screwed when you lose your queen. It's not like when you lose your king which just means the game is over. When you lose your queen, you have to spend the rest of your game worrying, and having to worry while you play is worse than not playing at all. Spike stands up and tries to pry the plastic lady out of my hand. Her hair is poking out everywhere because she's been thinking and when Spike thinks she likes to rake her fingers through her hair. She's pissed and puffed-up and I think I see her eyes turning from blue to yellow like they're burning something off. I've never seen her mad like this and between that and her hair, all of a sudden I start to laugh and can't stop. Then I feel a big strong hand on mine and I realize it's the guy I was thinking reminded me of God, so I stop laughing and relinquish the queen.

Spike and me are stone-still, who knows what homeless people do when you wreck their chess game. But the guy sits back down and rolls the queen between his thumb and index finger, and then he says this: You know what I like to do when I get all tense like you two girlies, I like to go out and perform what I call "action poems." Like what? we want to know. Like tripping ladies in fur coats, he says, or depositing a burning butt into the night-drop at the bank. Spike and me get all quiet, thinking about how great this is, and Spike makes up one of her own: How about pissing on a Mercedes? I smack Spike for pretending like she has a dick, but this time we all think it's funny. Spike and I decide that this guy has made our night and we realize that everyone but us has gone to bed, so we say good night and leave this guy and I say Spike, we have met one really excellent homeless person.

Spike and I lay next to each other on the blue-speckled carpet and listen to the other people breathe. Why do all these homeless people have to breathe so goddamn loud. It's worse than crickets. Spike keeps trying to spoon me and I keep kicking her out of my crooks, but Spike's persistent and I decide to let her put her hand up my shirt, that way she'll keep still. She thinks that if she moves I'll kick her away again. I don't think I will tonight though. I don't know why not. That pisses me off because I don't like not knowing things. I can feel Spike using all her might not to fidget, and my brain's all clear, way too clear for me to handle, much less sleep, so I say Spikey, let's hit the road, let's drive all night until the 7-11 decides it's Monday and get ourselves a six-pack.

SOMETHING WILL GROW

I HAVE THIS LITTLE GIRL THAT I TAKE CARE OF NOW. ERIKA, and only today did she snag on me and make me think that my daughter would have been just her size by now. Big enough to fight and think an original thought. Six years old. I had Erika in the shower, she looked like she could use a wash, and while I'm soaping up her tight, flat belly she turns around and starts soaping mine and right there was the snag.

The plumbing was clogged with our hair so that soap bubbles caught in the drain. It looked like someone had poured caviar down it, little marbles with a mother-of-pearl gleam. That was how James Ho's sperm came into me, like streams of little bubbles, and my egg sucked them up until it burst out an embryo, a little girl. I don't like to think that it might have been a boy. A little replica of James Ho's body, that body he foisted on me like too many sweets. It was sweet, it was, and I wanted it. James's body was even sweeter than Erika's, which is still young enough for me to scrub, lather over like a seal baby, all brown and slim.

If it had been a boy James Ho's parents might have even been secretly pleased, and forgiven James for bringing home the girl who was not only white, but too young for them to know if he could beat her on the SAT's. "How old are you, Lanie?" I was young enough to reach across the dinner table to grab my brother by the hair and for him to retaliate by pouring milk into my dinner plate. "Fifteen." I was hot under my arms. My heart tilting. I wanted them to like me.

"She's very mature for her age," James said to his parents, with scripted sarcasm. Then he took me upstairs and we had sex in his bedroom with the door locked. I let my voice be heard that day, with his parents downstairs, knowing I was mature for my age, wanting them to know. I understood pleasure. I attacked it at the throat and it fought back. I did know more than other girls.

I had to throw my stockings away because James had come all over them. "Just leave them in the garbage can," he told me. "But won't your mother see them?" I asked, and he told me not to worry about it, and because he told me not to I didn't. I walked barelegged out the door past Mrs. Ho, who looked right down where my blue tights had been, and I said "It was nice meeting you," with my sweet-girl smile.

"Your mother hated me," I said when we were outside.

James sputtered. "Probably. What did you expect, Lanie?"

He did have a body, James Ho. All sinewy muscles that flexed far beyond my expectations. He spiraled his loving arms around me like they were custom made for my rib cage, but what did I know? I was only fourteen.

It's not Erika's size that matters so much. Not the number of years she has left before she turns into what I was when I knew James

Ho, not the number of years she has been real flesh. It's that I love her. Those rubbery limbs that attach themselves to me, the blank brown skin blushed at the cheeks. How little it takes to love. The way she says my name, Lanie. How she tries to twist away from me but laughs as I dry her off with an old, soft towel and she runs, she screams. The Big Sister program would take her away from me if they knew I did this, but I've never been able to follow other people's rules when they deprive me of joy.

As I'm holding Erika she brings her hand to her mouth. "Look, Lanie," she says, and wiggles a tooth. It's loose. "Jiggle it," she says. I feel the heat of her breath as I wag the tooth to and fro, and suddenly it snaps off soundlessly, comes clean in my fingers. "Erika," I gasp, "you've lost another tooth!" It's her second one, tiny, ridged along the top. I ask her if she wants to take it home for the Tooth Fairy but Erika just looks at me, wrinkling her forehead like I've said something strange, and runs away again, squealing, wanting me to chase her. I'm left with the tooth in my hand and I think about Erika's family, immigrants from a culture where a tooth is just a tooth. I put it in my pocket. Erika is naked in the living room, the towel abandoned on the floor.

"Come get me Lanie," she taunts, wanting me to catch her, ready to run.

No one ever saw me naked like this, no one until James Ho. When I go to Erika's apartment to pick her up, her little brother is curled up on the couch in nothing but purple nylon underwear, always the same ones, and Erika in white cotton. Her mother makes her get dressed before she leaves with me, looking bashful, but not because her children are bare. Erika runs away from me as I chase her, and I pick the wet, limp towel off of the floor. I hold the towel up like a cape as I run after her, in case she wants to run into it and have me wrap her up.

I once let James Ho strip me down, get me naked in the park. He wanted to see what it would do to me, being that naked in a place where stranger witnesses might come along, if I would have a voice. That was the time we couldn't bother with condoms, and five weeks later, when all I wanted was the ability to do nothing, my little daughter wouldn't just go away. He took me, he was upstairs in the waiting room watching *The Pursuit of Happyness* while she got sucked out of me, and then he dropped me home. After that I never wanted to see him again, and he called and called, but by then all I wanted was for James Ho to die.

James Ho did die, actually. He killed himself in the middle of Harvard.

The news was delivered to me by phone, by an awed schoolmate. Many people were taken aback by James Ho's self-annihilation. Some took it personally. Few from our world made it to the Ivy League; most of us hoped for two years at community college, followed by state schools. For those of struggling with the tangles of life, James Ho seemed to be ahead of us, swinging a scythe. But I couldn't say I was surprised. I knew him. James was never happy. That's why he would back me up against the wall at school and say all melancholy, "If only you weren't so short, Lanie, you would be so beautiful. If only your legs were longer..." If only. James wanted everything in the world to be perfect but he knew he didn't deserve it. It was the only way he could cope, settling for things and then trying to improve them.

The teachers were all tiptoes around me that day, the day everyone found out. They'd seen us kissing in the hallway, by the lockers, years before. Twice we'd been caught after school, in the health classroom with the lights off. They remembered. But they didn't know. They didn't know how James Ho's touch could nearly tip me off the edge of my red brain. That if it hadn't been him, it would've been someone else. I was glad he was dead, and they didn't know that either. When Mr. Schwartz, the math teacher, stopped me on my way out of the cafeteria to ask if I was okay, I said "Yes Mr. Schwartz, I am absolutely fine." I walked away and left him in the wake of my relief.

James Ho had swallowed a bottle of pills, died the cowardly way. He washed them down with a Diet Coke and slept my secrets away.

Erika looks nothing like my daughter would have looked. She's brown and her eyes are big spoonfuls of innocence, not the confused slant my daughter would have had. When I take her back home, she flings herself into her mother's big arms, and says "Mami, Mami." But this look of alarm takes over her face as I turn to walk out the door, and she runs back to me, jumps in my arms, says "Lanie, don't go away." And for the first time in years, since James Ho died, I hate him not for what he gave me, but for what he took away. I carry Erika back to her mami and drop her gently in her lap. When they look up at me right before I leave, I see their faces turn identical the moment that they smile. James Ho's face was the only memory of my daughter, the only image.

I close myself into the long, dim hallway and walk towards the stairwell, slipping my hands into my pockets. My feet are heavy as my blood had stopped circulating and collected at my lowest points. But then I feel the tooth nestled in pocket lint, the sharp, hollow end pressing into my fingertip. I pinch it between my finger and thumb, this small, disposable child-bone. I rub the tooth like a charm; I can't help thinking that if I plant it somewhere, something will grow.

THIRTY SECONDS

THE FACT THAT JOHNNY KIRK IS DEAD HAS LITTLE TO DO WITH ME. My hours were officially over at six o'clock that day, and the only reason I was at the Country Club with the Kirks at six thirty-five, when it happened, was because I'm nice. And now I am officially not the Kirks' babysitter anymore, even though I'm sure it's not because Mr. Kirk thinks I was in any way responsible, because I wasn't, and anyway he has clearly decided who to blame.

I handled it well, I thought. I took Isabelle to my house after they took Johnny away in the ambulance, and I didn't expect them to pay me. Isabelle didn't understand what had happened so I slid *The Little Mermaid* into the DVD player and hoped she wouldn't ask me where her parents and brother were or why they weren't going to the Blackwells' for dinner like they were supposed to. All she wanted to know was if I had Sun Chips. No, I told her, *my* mother doesn't allow junkfood in the house.

So Johnny is dead and never again will he whip it out and say "This is my penis" with his big proud grin. He did that every day to me, and every day I would say, "I know Jonathan, put it back in your pants." I told Mrs. Kirk after he began doing this on a regular basis, because I didn't know if there was something I was supposed to do about it, but all she did was say "That Johnny," looking, I thought, a little proud with her thin, tight grin.

Mrs. Kirk is unlike most of the ladies I know from the Country Club. I've been a Guest there since fourth grade because my friend Stacy is a Member and she's always brought me along; she's the one who hooked me up with the babysitting gig with the Kirks. Mrs. Kirk is younger than Mr. Kirk, but I think what makes it harder for her to fit in is her bleach-blond hair and orangey skin, when all the other Country Club ladies have hair that's supposed to look like it's a natural color even if it isn't, and hide their faces from the sun with baseball hats embroidered with the names of their kids' boarding schools. Every morning I come over at nine and she goes off in her Lexus SUV to do something called Zumba. She comes back in a great mood, sweaty and jazzed in her exercise clothes. Sometimes she goes directly upstairs and shuts herself in the bedroom suite playing Shakira songs. I think I'm supposed to believe that she's taking her shower the whole time, but I hear the thuds on the ceiling above where Isabelle and I play and I know Mrs. Kirk is working out her Zumba moves. Sometimes, I fantasize about walking in there without knocking to catch her in the act, but then I picture her horrified O of a mouth and I feel bad for being the kind of person who has fantasies like that.

For the rest of the day her mood droops like the pansies in the front garden when she forgets to water them. When we go to the pool for lunch, her expressions get fake like her hair and the only thing that makes her light up is the sight of Isabelle or Johnny, but only after she hasn't seen them for a while.

The last time I saw Mrs. Kirk smile was in the locker room at the Country Club, and I doubt she's smiled since then. I was changing Isabelle out of her bathing suit and into her clothes. This is an elaborate and time-consuming process because Isabelle inevitably needs to tinkle at the point where I get her completely naked, so I have to bring her into a stall, and I let her sit down right on the seat even though I never would myself—even those Country Club people might have crabs—but I know Mrs. Kirk never puts paper down for her either, so. Then she always decides that she'd rather be naked than clothed and I have to chase her all over the locker room, bring her back to where we started, and then try to shove her limbs through the holes in her shorts and shirt. I was at this part, trying to get her arm unbent so I could get her t-shirt on, when Mrs. Kirk came into the locker room.

I was very annoyed at this point. It was already six-thirty and I was supposed to meet Catch at Pizzeria Uno at six fifteen. The Kirks were late for a barbecue at the Blackwells', too, and Mrs. Kirk gave us one of those smiles as she stuck her head in the door and said "What's taking you so long darling?"

I looked up at her, trying not to appear irritated, and smiled hopelessly.

"I don't want to wear a shirt," Isabelle whined. "I only want the shorts and nooooooooo shoes."

Mrs. Kirk laughed and said "Okay honey, you can wear just your shorts home in the car, but when we go to the Blackwells' you're going to have to put on a shirt."

Isabelle started to cry. Mrs. Kirk gave me a what-can-you-do eyeroll, went out the door, and I gratefully shoved the t-shirt into her bag.

I was thinking about trying to call Catch to see if he was still home so I could tell him I'd be late. But I didn't have a cell phone and I didn't like to ask to borrow Mrs. Kirk's. He was going to be pissed. He probably hadn't been able to borrow his father's car and had walked. I was thinking about his red-mad face when Mrs. Kirk ran back into the locker room and asked, all concerned, "Have you seen Johnny? Is Johnny in here?" I told her no. I tried to look concerned too, but Mrs. Kirk got frantic when it came to her kids sometimes and I figured that Johnny had just wandered into the snack bar or the parking lot. I picked up Isabelle, as clothed as she was going to get, slung the pool-bag over my shoulder, and went outside.

Hedges surrounded the pool grounds, and Mrs. Kirk was looking behind them one at a time, her blonde head bobbing all over the place. She kept calling his name. I guess she thought he was hiding, which would have been a typical thing for Jonathan to do. I could picture him crouched behind the very last place his mother would look, little snickers of joy sneaking out past the fist in his mouth. "Where's Johnny?" Isabelle asked me. "He's around here somewhere," I said. Isabelle can be really cute. She looked up at me with her huge brown eyes—a really cute kid, and sweet too, not like Jonathan. Jonathan had already learned, probably from his father now that I think about it, how to be an asshole, and he was only five and a half. He was a hitter. It made me so mad when he hit Isabelle. She would cry and never hit back, and he would look up at me all proud of himself, and then hit her again and she'd cry harder. Sometimes I really wanted to slug him back, but of course babysitters can't do that, so I'd grab him by the arm and say "Jonathan, it's not nice to hit your sister. How would you like it if someone bigger than you and stronger than you hit you?" And he'd always look at me like he was all hurt, like how could I do this to him, but I was doing the right thing, wasn't I? I thought I was doing better than his parents, who sort of said, "Jonathan, bad boy," like he was a dog. He listened to his father if he ever said anything, but Mr. Kirk was never around much.

Mr. Kirk scared me to death. He drove me home in his sedan if I had to sit late. I liked the car, it had this great smell to it which I think was the leather, but Mr. Kirk never talked to me at all. There was one time when I was riding home with him, and I'd forgotten that I'd taken my bra off while I was watching TV, after Isabelle and Johnny had gone to sleep, and stuffed it in my purse. So I was conscious of my breasts, even though they're small, bouncing around on the bumpy road. I folded my arms under them for support, but it felt awkward so I put my hand down on the seat and it accidentally landed partially on top of Mr. Kirk's. I said "oops, sorry," in reflex, and he gave me this weird look, like he was startled and annoyed at the same time. But he didn't say anything. Not even "it's okay." I sighed, and he sighed, and we drove home in silence except for the squeaking the leather made as I squirmed in my seat.

Otherwise I never saw him, if he was in the house he was upstairs in his bedroom or his study, both of which I figured were off-limits to me, and the rest of the time he was either working or at the Golf Club. I still don't know what his job is. Mrs. Kirk told me one time that it was Re-insurance I think, but I don't know what that could mean. Anyway he really loved Johnny. He got this tough-voice with him, he'd say, "How's my man" and Johnny would give him five. But he never changed Isabelle's diapers, and as soon as a temper tantrum showed signs of brewing, he looked at me or his wife like, your turn. I think secretly he wanted Johnny to hit Isabelle, so he'd be able to feel who's boss. All siblings beat on each other, right? Like it's the big brother's job.

But Isabelle loved Johnny, no matter how much he smacked her or stole her Sun Chips or grabbed the pegs out of her Lite Brite just to be mean. She was looking around at her mother, who was looking for Jonathan, and she asked it again: "Where's Johnny?" Mrs. Kirk's eyes had gone savage. She had enlisted the help of the pool guy and she was firing questions at him: "Do you think he could've gone out the gate?" she asked. "Do you think he's hiding in the men's room?" she asked, but the pool guy went in and checked all the stalls and he wasn't hiding. "Do you think he walked to the car?" she asked, but Jonathan would never do that, even I knew that, he would never go far away from his mother, he NEEDED her. So it occurred to me and I asked the question to myself: Do you think he's in the pool? But of course he wasn't in the pool. They would've checked there by now anyway, I thought, but there was no way he was in the pool, Mrs. Kirk was only in the locker room for less than thirty seconds, how could he be in the pool? So I looked because I knew he wouldn't be there. But then I saw, in the corner of the deep end, a wobbly black blur.

I let out a weird loud sound that didn't seem to come from me and I almost dropped Isabelle, and the pool guy must have seen where I was looking because he dove right in even though he was near the shallow-end. Mrs. Kirk dropped her purse and she dove in, yelling things, My God My God, and I thought that Isabelle really shouldn't see this, she really shouldn't see this, so I carried her over to the other side of the poolhouse where the phone was. I dialed 911 and I told them yes, this was an emergency, there's a little kid on the bottom of the pool.

Catch was so mad at me he pretended like he wasn't ever going to talk to me again. I called him up and he just sat there on the other end of the phone, breathing in my ear. He felt kind of stupid when I told him that Johnny, the kid I babysat, was in a coma, and I told it all tragically to make him feel stupider. "Are you okay?" he asked. "Yeah, I'm okay," I said. "Are they going to sue the Country Club?" he asked, but I told him I didn't think so given that the Country Club was their life, and anyway the pool officially closed at six so technically they were trespassing. So Catch said he'd take me out to a better dinner than Pizzeria Uno the next day. He felt bad for me. I told him that really, he shouldn't feel bad for me. But I wasn't going to complain about getting taken out to dinner—Catch never took me out. I always paid for myself, which I think is fair, and the Kirks paid me twelve dollars an hour so it wasn't like I didn't have any money.

*

Isabelle began to catch on after *The Little Mermaid* was over. I tried to get her to watch it again, but she was beginning to wonder what she was doing in my house, and where her parents were and she'd seen the *The Little Mermaid* three thousand times so it was no longer interesting enough to keep her mind off other things. So I told her, "Johnny hurt himself so Mommy and Daddy took him to see a doctor." I figured that was harmless yet honest. "What part of himself did he hurt?" she asked. "Uhhh..." I said. What should I have told her, he hurt his brain? He hurt his lungs, his heart? "He hurt his head," I said, feeling a little like I was cheating, but Isabelle accepted that and then forgot. She plucked a burnt sienna from my box of Crayolas and went off into another world. Little kids are great with that.

Catch said his father would let him borrow the car so he could take me and Isabelle to the hospital. It was nice of him but it wasn't like he could really say no. Catch was surprisingly good with Isabelle and she giggled all the way to the hospital, wedged between me and Catch on the long bench seat even though that was definitely illegal. "My ass has never once known a car seat and I'm still alive," Catch told me when he lifted her into the front seat. "What's your favorite color?" he asked Isabelle, more excited than I've ever heard him in my life. "Pink and purple swirl," she said. "Pink and purple swirl!" said Catch, "That's not a color, that's two colors, you're cheating. Pick one." "Pinkish purple," she said, and giggled. She had a crush on him bad by the time we pulled up to the hospital, which to be honest with you made me a little jealous. I picked her up out of the car, and she said "Are we going to see Mommy and Johnny?" "Yes," I said, "And Daddy too." Which gives you an idea of how much she expected to see her Daddy.

But he was there. Of course he was there. I was the one who had called the clubhouse, where they tracked him down in that room where women are only allowed on Sundays. I told them to tell Mr. Kirk that it was an emergency and he should come to the pool right away. Maybe I should've talked to him myself, but what was I supposed to say? "I think Johnny might be dead"? He came right over, anyway. He had someone drive him over in a golf cart, and as soon as he saw what was going on he panicked. I've never seen Mr. Kirk anything like this before. He ran across the bricks even though he was still in his golf shoes, he clack-clack-clacked all the way over to the corner of the pool where Johnny, Mrs. Kirk, and the pool guy were, all of them soaked, Johnny unconscious and limp. Mrs. Kirk was holding him and really crying. I heard the ambulance pull up. Luckily I had left Isabelle on the other side of the pool house, examining the contents of her sticker kit. "Stay there, Isabelle," I would say if she looked like she was going to come over to me, and she stayed, even though she really wanted to know what was going on. Johnny would have come to me just because I told him not to.

Mr. Kirk pushed his wife and the pool guy away and grabbed onto Johnny, and I heard him say over and over again, "My son, my son, my son, my son." I had never seen one hint of emotion on this man's face before, not even one of those smiles you give to people just to be nice. Right then his face was all twisted up. He was crying. He really scared me.

*

Johnny must've died right when we got to the hospital because we walked in on a really bad scene. From down the hall I could hear Mr. Kirk screaming. "You had one thing to do!" His voice cracked. "You had one reason to live!" Catch and I shuffled. We looked at each other and I let him know by the thinning of my lips that yes, that was Mr. Kirk. Isabelle's body twisted toward the voices of her parents. I hoped she didn't know that it was her father, it really didn't sound like him. But then she knew for sure, because I guess the doctors wanted them out and the Kirks came into the hallway with a lady doctor who was simultaneously trying to get Mr. Kirk away from Mrs. Kirk and get them out of the room. His face was all red. His hair was a mess and so was Mrs. Kirk's. His hands flapped in the air. "FAILURE, FAILURE!" he screamed. By then Isabelle let out a good long wail and had closed her eyes. I guess she didn't know where to look, but I couldn't take my eyes off the commotion.

Catch raised his eyebrows as if asking me a question I was supposed to have the answer to. I didn't know what to do. How was I supposed to know what to do? My parents had their share of fights but I had never, ever in real life even imagined something like this happening. Maybe behind closed doors. That was what I couldn't believe, that it was in front of strangers, in front of doctors and their daughter, and me. He looked over to where I was standing, holding his daughter, and he suddenly stopped. Isabelle had her head thrown back and her mouth open like a hungry baby bird. At first there was no sound, then a shriek of despair poured out of Isabelle's mouth and flooded the hospital hall. Mr. Kirk straightened up, turned, and as if back to his old self, took Isabelle from my arms and held her in a fatherly hug as she clung to him like a little monkey.

Mrs. Kirk reached into her purse and retrieved the elastic headband she wore to Zumba. She pulled it down around her neck, then carefully pushed it back against her bleach-blond hair. Her eyes were the kind of dead that looks like it's forever.

I still don't know what happened. All Mrs. Kirk did was come into the locker room and tell Isabelle she didn't have to wear her shirt. I've repeated everything we said that day and timed it, using the second hand on my watch. It couldn't have been more than thirty seconds. The pool guy was out there, what happened? Why wasn't there a splash, why didn't he thrash around? I don't know, but I've got other things to worry about now. My two best friends are barely in touch because I have no way to text and school is starting soon. Plus the fact that I don't have a job anymore. Mr. Kirk called me up, as if nothing had ever happened that day in the hospital, and told me that they would no longer be needing a babysitter. He thanked me for taking care of Isabelle on "the day of the tragedy," he said, and hung up. But I was a good babysitter, I think. No one ever swallowed pennies or ate the crayons, not while I was looking after them.

FREAKS

YOU FIRST NOTICED THE SCALES WHEN YOU WERE TWELVE YEARS old. They appeared flesh-colored, on your right arm, like sunburn peeling, and since it was summer and you had been spending way too much time at the pool, your parents didn't seem alarmed. They started in a small patch in the middle of your forearm, halfway between your hand and your elbow. You could camouflage them with your left hand. Your mother rubbed Nivea lotion on them and had you stay out of the sun. After a week, your tan had faded and the scales were gone. Six weeks later they came back, and their residence was twice as long, and the third time they tendriled around your wrist you were not surprised to see them.

Sometimes months passed between flare-ups. Episodes lasted two to fifteen days. The right forearm was the only zone in which they appeared. When you were fourteen, during an episode in which the scales were particularly reflective and plum-toned, your mother finally said, "Let's get you to the doctor." She wrapped an ace bandage around your arm and secured it with safety pins in case you ran into someone you knew at the doctor's office.

"Psoriasis," Dr. Abraham said. He was your pediatrician. He

examined your nails. You had painted them with Really Red nail polish and he had to borrow his secretary's nail polish remover to take it off. "The nails look fine," he said, and checked your scalp, as if looking for lice, but found nothing unusual aside from the patch on your right arm. "They're a strange color, these scales," Dr. Abraham told your mother, and he prescribed synthetic vitamin D, tar, and recommended that your mother buy a sunlamp.

You rubbed coal tar on your arm. It was sticky and black and strands of your long, brown hair got stuck in it when you leaned over. You sat under a sunlamp for thirty minutes a day, and the scales spread, reaching almost down to your Swatch and approaching the elbow. On your second visit to Dr. Abraham he addressed your mother as you sat, uncomfortably slumped, on the examination table. "I've never seen psoriasis like this, not even in a textbook. Her skin is almost purple. I have a friend who's a dermatologist; you should go see him."

"That's some psoriasis," the dermatologist said, and prescribed some cortisone cream. The cream didn't do anything for the scales, but you did grow addicted to it, and soon the skin around the scales, the normal human skin, began to require that cortisone cream so that it became red and itchy and angry if its needs weren't met. He tried cortisone shots anyway, injected them right into the scaly area, pushing through the thickened skin in a way that reminded you of how you used to stick thumbtacks into the vinyl couch. The injections bruised the normal skin; the scales were unaffected. The third doctor observed you with a series of emotional reactions you were beginning to recognize as a sequence: first confused; then earnest in examination; finally, detached. This was a medium-sized suburban town in New Jersey, the kind of town doctors settled in to enjoy their lives. Doctors here were not interested in the challenge of a tough case. They lived in the biggest of the box-like houses that made artificial rings around what was once farmland and engaged actively in their hobbies. "Is it psoriasis?" asked your mother. "No," he said. "This is not psoriasis and to be honest I don't know what this is." He held the weight of your arm in his latex-gloved hand, shaking his head, subtly flabbergasted. You never asked questions. You didn't want to deal with the finer points of this condition any more than the doctors did.

He told you to go cold turkey with the cortisone, and to take baths with baking soda. He didn't advise you to make a follow-up visit. After two more dermatologists failed to make a diagnosis, you planned your daily wardrobe around the length of your sleeves. In the summers you wore gauzy, white men's shirts with the buttons undone. Your friends quickly learned not to ask, "Aren't you boiling?"

Of course, your friends knew about the scales. You knew they even allowed themselves to shudder and thank God they didn't have them. They had problems enough to worry about without a physical deformity of unknown origin. Kristen was anorexic; Janie had stress-induced insomnia that was the result of her fear of not getting into Cornell; Veronica had gotten drunk last weekend and accidentally lost her virginity to David Drake, one of the school's biggest assholes. Many had eating disorders—those were the rexies—but Kristen was in her own league, the only one who earned the full word. Kristen had gone from 135 pounds to 98 in a matter of six months. The boys found Kristen somewhat grotesque, but the girls mostly envied her, especially the rexies, even while they talked behind her back, saying "Poor Kristen. She's so fucked up," out of revenge.

No one envied you, though. No one wanted an arm that looked like it belonged in the reptile house at the zoo. Your father told you, "Looks don't matter, Emiline. Someone will love you for what's inside." But "looks don't matter" was a lie the rexies told each other as they tried to get an edge on their competition, encouraging their friends to eat more.

All you could do was accept the social rules of your environment. You studied diligently and kept your mouth shut about the A's you got, not that everyone didn't know everyone else's grades anyway; they posted the names of the students who made Honor Roll and High Honor Roll on the door of the principal's office every quarter, as a means of incentive. You wore sweaters and pulled the right sleeve down, holding it in your fist. You ducked from boys, and David Drake ignored you—a small perk.

Then, when you were sixteen, you contracted mononucleosis and missed a month of school. You lay prone for days, mute from a secondary throat infection, and took to running the fingers from your left hand over the scales on your right arm. In a moment of brain-soft falling consciousness, your fingers told your sensory receptors that the sensation of being against those scales was good. Compared to your throat, which harbored white pus and cramped horribly, the scales seemed to be the healthiest part of you. They were smooth and clean. The tough purple shine flourished as the rest of your body lay in temporary decay. Similarly, you reframed the way you considered the hair that had grown under your arms while you felt too weak to shower. You decided to refrain from shaving even after you got better.

When you went back to school, you arrived in a black pocket t-shirt that you'd stuck in the back of your shirt drawer reserved for times of remission. It was the end of April, just getting warm. You hung your jean jacket in your locker before the first bell rang. You had never shown this much skin at school, not even when you changed for gym class; you always changed in a bathroom stall while everyone else compared "muffin tops" in the communal changing room. It was clear to those who had lockers near yours—Jordan Rosen froze mid-locker combination as you clamped your own lock shut—that you had made a decision. Your friends were suspicious. They wanted to know, they knew you couldn't change the fact that you had some weird skin disease, but WHY IN THE HELL DID YOU STOP SHAVING YOUR PITS, EMILINE? That was just bad taste.

They asked a question other than the one they wanted the answer to. "Aren't you chilly, Emiline?" Janie asked.

"A little," you said.

"So why are you wearing a short-sleeved shirt, huh Em?"

"I guess I just feel like it," you said, and Janie glanced nervously at Jill. The other girls sitting at the lunchtime hangout bench looked down at their laps. Erica said, "Dude." And Kristen, sitting next to them, eating dry lettuce out of a plastic bag, watched you in utter fascination.

You became friends with Kristen, this rabbity wraith who

always seemed so stable and poised despite the problem that everyone knew she had. Kristen held a high social position due to unconditional friendliness, a solid academic record and a history of a childhood tucked smartly into Ralph Lauren ensembles. No one talked to her about her weight, not even her parents anymore, you heard, but Kristen knew that everyone was always talking about her.

"You know, they're jealous of you," you told her.

"They wouldn't be if they could see this," Kristen told you. She lifted up her shirt. You were over at her house, sitting on her bed. A bag of sugar candy lay open on the bedspread, spilling out. With her loose t-shirt raised above her belly, you could see pale pink skin sucking over an elaborate instrument made of bones—more bones than you realized a body could have. But this isn't what Kristen was showing you; she was showing you the fur that grew on the skin. All over her belly: dark brown down. You had heard that this happened to anorexics, that their bodies grew fur when they had no fat to keep them warm. "You can touch it," she told you, and you did. It was soft and animal. You let her touch your scales in return. "My God," she said. "It's so smooth and dry. Not slimy at all. It feels amazing, Em."

You and Kristen began spending your lunches together. She explained to you that she ate lettuce because it had no calories, and the sugar candy was for energy; it had no fat. Occasionally, she liked to eat plain sprinkles, which she would filch from the ice cream sundae bar they had for dessert at school lunches. She would never eat chocolate, though. Very rarely, she craved protein and then she would eat baked chicken or an egg. You bought her gummy peaches and gummy worms and hard candies. Her teeth were yellowish and rotting. Though you didn't like feeling responsible for this, you reasoned it was better for her to be eating sugar candy than nothing at all. She lost a few more pounds, but didn't seem concerned.

"What does it feel like, never eating?" you asked her once. You were sitting at Smithies, downtown, where you and your friends flocked because it had the best cheeseburgers in town. The rexies claimed it also had the best fat-free Caesar salad dressing. Kristen fished the lemon out of her water glass and sucked on cubes of ice while you savored bites of melted cheese and rich animal fat and the lovely tang of ketchup. When you'd had mono, you couldn't eat for three days; you could barely get spit down your throat. The morning your mother brought you chocolate pudding and you could finally taste it on your tongue without fear, little sparks of joy lifted the corners of your mouth. You were overwhelmed with wonderment, watching Kristen push cubes of ice into the hollows of her cheeks, sucking up the smallest sips of water to test her ability to make the portion last. How did Kristen have such strength? "How does it feel," you asked, dipping a fry in ketchup, "to sit here and watch me eat something I enjoy so much?"

Kristen never seemed affected by the food that other people ate, as if it were separate from her, but the question was not well-received that day. She dropped her spoon on the table and it clattered. "What does it feel like, having an arm that people mistake for a pet python?"

Your lips parted and your breath came in an involuntary inward suck. Kristen had never said anything like this before. Her expression changed into one of remorse. "I'm sorry, Em," she said. "I feel cranky today."

"That's okay, I understand," you said. You gave her the kind of grave look people gave each other on television. You said, "That happens when you don't eat."

She looked at you, sunken eyes wide, and then you both broke out in cackles. You laughed so hard that the waitress came over to bring you the check and was so confused by these two freakish teenage girls, one a skeleton with skin, the other with some nasty skin condition that was even more horrible than the eczema one supposed it was from far away, giggling like normal teenage girls that she tossed the check onto the table and fled. You tipped her twenty percent anyway. You and Kristen walked out of the restaurant and onto Fairfield Avenue, bony arm in scaly arm, and laughed away the notion that some people are just simple. Let them flee.

You were opposites in some ways, you and Kristen. For starters, lust kicked in for you. Kristen reported being entirely bored by the idea of sex.

"I know it's a cliché," said Kristen. "But boys are really stupid. Anyway, I don't like for people to touch my body." Not that anyone wanted to touch Kristen's body the way it was now, except for you. There was a time, when she was first losing the weight, when boys would incite mass jealousy among the other girls, when you would overhear them saying, "Kristen looks really hot. She's suddenly very fuckable." But that brief era came and went, and the boys shuddered at her now. She reminded them of death, of decay. She held too much power in things that no one else had. Self-control. Denial.

But suddenly boys seemed interested in you. They liked that you were different, perhaps grotesque, and confident anyway. So few girls had confidence. The boys were bored with saying "you're not fat" to girls who weren't fat; they were tired of saying "yes, I swear I really like you" to girls they didn't really like. You had once been like those girls, though you would never have asked anyone to reassure you that your scales were not ugly and horrible; you knew that they were. But since you had become friends with Kristen you'd taken on a new approach to people you didn't know. Strangers were offered your bare, scaled arm, as if you were reaching out to shake their hand. If they flinched, you walked off without a word. It became a challenge to the boys who had always known who you were, but had never spoken to you, to meet you without inspiring your disdain.

You landed one of the most desirable boys in school. It's not like you didn't have a pretty face. Many people said, "if only she didn't have those scales, she would be beautiful. And she gets straight A's, too." At a party at Tabitha's house, the boy named Victor squeezed himself into the overstuffed chair in which you were already sitting and told you you looked bored. You said, "I guess I am," even though you weren't; you had friends to talk to and were enjoying watching Ken Morrone get drunk and lean on girls. To your surprise, Victor stationed himself in the overstuffed chair for the duration of the party and attempted to rescue you from your alleged boredom. Victor was older, a handsome senior. Olive skin. Green eyes and black lashes, long lashes for a boy. Black hair growing out, you remembered a time when it used to be short, now it curled around his ears. You periodically glanced around to see if everyone was as amazed by his attention as you were. You checked out the kitchen, ate some Doritos, split a Schlitz. Neither of you were big drinkers and you laughed together as Ken Morrone puked into the bushes after too many rum & Diet Rites. You were intoxicated by something else, something crawling under your skin, all the way from your neck to the soles of your feet. It was lust. You mistook it for happiness. At the end of the night you sat Indian-style, facing each other, playing with the fringe on Tabitha's bedspread until Tabitha passed out on top of the bed and Victor offered to drive you home.

Victor came over three nights later. Your mother was so pleased to have a boy in the house, a boy that good-looking, that she allowed you to go into the bedroom and shut the door—something that most girls' mothers prohibited—and she must have known what was going on when you turned up the stereo. Victor knew he had you the moment he put his mouth on your neck and you leaned back and gasped. Still, he took his time crossing the line, and by the time he finally did reach between your legs, he could feel how wet you were through your jeans. Your eyes were open the whole time. You never blinked.

You weren't old enough for a driver's license and he couldn't often borrow his parents' car. On Saturdays he walked forty-five minutes to your house and arrived sweaty and grinning. You were in love with his energy, his hands, the teeth that flashed when he smiled. Victor had been with other girls, but he told you, as he rested his hand on your bare stomach, that you were different.

"How?" you asked him. "You aren't scared of things," he said, and moved back down between your legs, licking where you knew it was already swollen and ready, an elastic band that needed to be snapped, and after all of the muscles in your body went soft and involuntary, he brought his face in line with yours. He kissed you hard on the mouth and you kissed him back, starving for the taste of your desire, like a snake biting its own tail.

You told Kristen what things were like with Victor, you presented the facts, you explained that sex lifted you out of your skin at the same time it put you more solidly inside your body than you had ever been before. She was interested in your stories but while you told them her shoulders would tense up and she would pull a stick of gum out of her pocket, place the stick of gum flat on her tongue, and play with the wrapper until it was a mess of little foil-and-paper balls.

"I wish I wanted that, but I don't," Kristen said.

Eventually, Victor graduated and went to college, as people from your school did. You cried on Kristen's shoulder, which was now about as comfortable as the corner of your desk. Kristen was still losing weight. She was down to 90, she said when you asked, which meant she weighed less than that. People were beginning to stare at her and she wore spandex to school every day, which made people think she was really fucking nuts. She let you touch her bones and you loved them, they were like handles, their ridges called out for someone to take hold. Her favorite was her collarbone. Your favorite was her hip. The fact that you had the same bone somewhere underneath your flesh amazed you. Her hipbones were like mountains and yours were like icebergs, two points barely jutting out.

"The biggest problem I have," said Kristen, "is that I have trouble sleeping. I can't get comfortable at night. The bed's too hard." You went with her to Bed, Bath and Beyond and bought her an egg crate mattress cover with your parents' credit card. Kristen didn't have any money. Her parents were so mad at her for being anorexic that they would only give her things she wanted when she ate something, and they didn't think candy counted. Kristen had stopped asking them for things.

Your scales started peeling off right after Victor left. They itched and you scratched and the new skin bled and scabbed. You grew moody and cranky, despite the fact that your skin was growing in normal again. "You should be pleased," your mother said after you snapped at her over nothing. "I don't understand, Emiline. Your scales are finally going away and all you do is complain about it itching." How could you explain to her that you WANTED those scales, how tired and heavy and humorless you felt the moment you started to shed? Your mother had been attending Mass twice a week, dragging your father along on Sundays, and seemed to have less to say to you these days. She'd stopped selling real estate and taken a clerical position in a tall office building, where she often stayed later than she needed to on evenings she did not attend Mass or her church book club. When you discovered that she was secretly attending a support group for families of children with disabilities, you didn't speak to her for five days.

Victor wrote you letters about college and about his new

girlfriend, Heather. You distrusted his judgment. You had never met a Heather you had liked. You lost interest in boys altogether while your scales were peeling off and even stopped touching yourself at night, instead looking up at the ceiling with a deliberately sardonic and wounded expression towards God, saying "why can't you just afford me this one, little, thing?" When they returned they were the color of your skin, then slowly turned dark red, and by the time they turned back to their full purple and spread over your entire forearm, like a sleeve, you were lying on the living room carpet with Carlos Ramirez, his teeth locked on your earlobe, the first of your senses obliterated, the next sense close behind.

Carlos was a year behind you in school. He wore his father's old Leica around his neck like an accessory, and one day you stopped him in the locker aisle and asked him what he took pictures of. "I'd like to take pictures of you," he said. You knew he said that to any girl who asked, but you sensed a sweetness behind his confidence. He photographed you in low light with grainy, high-speed film and collected the spent cylinders in a large Ziplock bag. "It's good to see yourself with some distance," he told you. "I want you to see yourself how I see you." He had a two-week waiting period before he developed a roll of film; he thought the delay in gratification aided objectivity. Carlos was new to photography and many of his shots were blown out or foggy with darkness, but you liked flipping through the chemical-smelling prints he made in the school's darkroom, observing the stranger of your self. He showed you how to work the dials on his analog machine. When you saw images of your own knees and feet, you imagined how Kristen would translate into photographs. You knew she would never let Carlos take these images from her. But if he did, there would be angles, sharp curves, and unexpected shadows, and everything that made a picture good.

Your friends were filling out college applications, Xeroxing the originals and using the photocopy for practice. "Where are you applying, Emiline?" your friends asked you. You wanted to go somewhere different from where you were. Where girls ate cream cheese and pizza and drank real Coke. Where boys didn't hang pictures of George Bush in their lockers or make Holocaust jokes, and no one studied business or economics. One night, as you were sifting through Carlos' collection of photography magazines, you slowed on a spread of women who were so pale they seemed to be ghosts. They were albino women. In each frame, a new woman with bottomless eyes stared right at you, unflinching. You wanted to be that whitest of women with a confronting gaze, forever unblinking. But then you realized that what you wanted more than that was to be the man behind the lens.

You flipped to the back of the magazine and read the artist's biography. It said he lived in Portland, Oregon. A self-portrait accompanied the written bio. The photographer had short black hair and austere, unsmiling lips. His arms were muscular and decorated with tattoos from his shoulders to his wrists. A snake twined around his shoulder, its tongue hissing towards the photographer's clavicle. You didn't care if this connection was cosmetic. Something had already clicked.

You researched this faraway city. There were colleges there, of course. College was the one reason they let you leave this place—at least, no one you knew of had ever tried anything else successfully. The only alternative to college, if recent history proved correct, was getting a job at the downtown shopping area or at a local law firm. When you were a freshman, the star of the high school musical had shocked everyone by forgoing college and taking a job at Cumberland Farms; the act had impressed no one and frightened many. You weren't a renegade with a statement to make. You just wanted to be with other freaks.

Kristen checked herself into the hospital two weeks before she was scheduled to leave for Yale. You stopped by her house on your way to the hospital to pick up her favorite books. To reach her bookshelves, you had to climb over all the neatly-folded piles of sheets and blankets and pillow shams that her parents had bought for her dorm room. A new mountain bike was propped against the closet door; they'd bought her that too. They operated on a fantasy that she had the strength of a normal girl, that she was still normal, but by this time, Kristen could not even walk.

Kristen lay there, an IV in her arm, her legs making thin ridges in the hospital sheet. You could see the knobs of her knees. Her hair was falling out.

The IV dripped and you sat on her bed and said, "I read this book, *The Best Little Girl in the World*, and it said that lots of anorexics pull their IVs out because they're afraid to gain weight."

"I read that book," Kristen said. "That book was like a handbook on how to be anorexic." She looked up at the IV, not with contempt. "See, this way, it's beyond my control. I still won't eat. I can't eat. It's not my fault I'm getting fat."

You asked her what happened, why she had checked herself in, had something happened? You knew she had stopped eating candy; she only chewed gum now. "My doctor told me the only reason I'm alive is because of the gum!" she said, amazed, amused. She looked away, she didn't like melodrama, she said "I just didn't want to die yet," and reached for the books you brought.

People from school came to visit Kristen, no longer jealous, all of them palpably terrified for her. She only had one regret, she told you after everyone had left. "I'm a walking cliché," she said, and started to cry.

You came back for the funeral. Everyone did. Jill and Janie drove back from Pennsylvania, and David Drake flew back from Wisconsin. Kristen had volunteered at community centers around the town; everyone loved her. Hordes of people clogged the cemetery. You stood at the congregation's margin and held a small automatic camera in front of your eye.

"Such a tragedy," friends and parents muttered. "She was so smart, and she was beautiful before she got so sick. If only she'd realized how beautiful she was." You wanted to shake them. Boys called her a cow before she started losing the weight. You'd heard the stories of her father pinching her hips, saying, "Now that's more than an inch."

As they lowered Kristen's body into the ground, you were overwhelmed with the thought that no one understood what had happened. Kristen died because she wanted to. There was no other way for her. You pushed up the right sleeve of your sweater and placed your left hand on the scales and imagined her hand there. The knuckles pressing in with the edgy force she couldn't prevent.

You took pictures. The teachers in the crowd shot confused, warning looks your way. This was not appropriate. You held your camera up to David Drake. His color had drained; he looked genuinely distressed. It was an expression you'd never seen on his face before, and you took the picture. You shot Goldie Nicholson, the underclass sexpot, in her diaphanous flower-print button-down shirt with nothing but a black lace bra underneath; you shot trampled grass under leather boots. The camera served as a buffer between you and what was happening, and you were grateful for the security of the metal machine.

Someone touched you on the arm. You looked up to see a girl from your school. She was familiar, but you didn't know her name. She stood with Robbie Rosenberg, who ran cross-country and sat in the back of your Latin class one year. He was so skinny he was barely there.

"Nice ink," the girl said. Acne scars made divots in her cheeks. She touched the outlined red star that decorated the underside of your left elbow. "You don't remember me, do you?" she said.

"Heather?" you tried. She smiled and nodded. She yanked at the collar of her black dress and showed you a network of branches that had been inked onto her skin. You thought of the way Kristen's blue veins crossed under her skin like sudden cracks in a field of ice.

You remembered Heather and Robbie. You, yourself, had never given them much consideration, even when they walked past you in the hallway, or sat in the booth behind you at Smithies, or when Heather was changing for gym in the stall next to you while everyone else compared muffin tops in the communal changing room.

You looked into Heather's eyes and had the sensation of being poked in the sternum with a finger. Freaks like you had been here all the while, as visible to you as ghosts; you had been too afraid to step outside the outline of the inner circle, and perhaps all that time the cage that trapped you had had an open gate.

"Listen," Heather said. "I think you need to put the camera down." She said it with concern, kindly, and over her shoulder you saw the reason for her warning. From the cluster of mourners, Kristen's mother had emerged; she strode towards you. Her straight brown hair was limp and flyaway. She wore the expression of an animal who wanted to devour you. Her eyes were cushioned by the bluish puffed skin beneath them, but they flashed hot with fury.

"You," she said. She pointed her finger. She began to gallop. "You think you see something no one else sees?" she called. Mourners turned to watch her progress towards you. Heather took a step away.

You dangled the camera by your side. You froze. You did nothing but watch the thing happen.

"YOU," the mother said, charging. "YOU. YOU."

HEATHENS

Molly, muñeca, my doll. I watch you flirting with Rudolfo, just across the road, and you pronounce his name the gringo way: *Rude-all-foe.* I've sent you over to the *pulpería* to buy me a ginger ale but it was only an excuse to get you over to where Rudolfo was, and you knew it. I simply wanted to observe. You come back without my ginger ale, all taken over with laughter because you don't speak any Spanish, and he doesn't speak any English, and all you've done is stand there smiling at each other like idiots. "He has lice," I tell you. "Oh my God," you say, face broken, and start raking your fingers through your hair. Rudolfo doesn't have lice but for some reason you believe everything I say. Rudolfo's over at the *pulpería* still periodically pursing his lips in your direction, but now you see him as nothing more than the peasant you first considered him to be.

"Do they all have lice?" you ask me.

"A lot of them do."

"Have you gotten it yet?" You look under your nails for bugs.

"No, I keep my hair pulled back and I don't get too close to them." Maybe this will keep you from picking up the kids. Maybe you'll tell the other gringos and they'll all keep their distance now.

"I got lice one year at camp," you say. "It was awful. My mother made me cut off all my hair." Those golden locks. Slippery as silk from corn, or from the bowels of worms.

You've been here for a week now, living with the other gringos in the minister's house. I don't know why you came *here*; I don't ask. I'm the one you all come running to for the answers, the gringa who actually, God forbid, lives here. You and the other girls came wearing long skirts and long sleeves and carrying Café Rica tote bags on your arms, designer coffee to bring home as a souvenir. One of the boys wore a t-shirt that said "I'm so glad I voted for Bush!" I saw you as I was on my way to school, a clot of gringos in the middle of the road, as if you'd just descended from a tour bus in order to see some monument. But there's no monument here, only a road, a school, a *pulpería* that serves Coca-Cola out of plastic bags. And of course a church, though the wrong kind for you. Your kind has no official house; the *evangelicos* here—their converts multiplying by the month—carry their cults from house to house each week, something certain Americans, your Americans, would like to see rectified.

I kept going, walking to school, hoping that none of you would see me. But you, Molly, saw me and thought I was a friend. Pale skin, blond hair, a dress from the bargain rack of Filene's Basement—all things you recognized. You ran over and stuck out your hand and when you withdrew it, it went to the gold cross around your neck.

"I hope you don't wear that while you're in San José," I told you.

"Why not?" you asked.

"It'll get ripped right off your neck. By the *chapulines*."

That, at least, was true. The *chapulines* rip gold necklaces off of people's necks all the time, especially gringo necks. Some of the facts I pass to you are actually useful. And when you come running to me for knowledge, I give it to you. Don't flush your toilet paper, it will clog the plumbing. Put it in the waste basket. Rice and beans are good for you and you will offend your hosts if you refuse it. Don't flirt too much with the boys or you'll be sorry.

As soon as I tell Jorge about you, he's interested. "Another gringa in town? In our humble little town?"

He picks up the end of my braid and fondles it. I squirm in the heat. The sweat has dampened my dress and my legs seem glued to the vinyl couch.

"A whole lot of gringas. But they're all Evangelical."

"Oh," he says. He drops my braid, then picks it back up off my shoulder and yanks it hard.

"Ow, *cabrón*," I say. He picks up my hand, kisses it, and afterwards, smiles.

Jorge's mother comes over from the kitchen and sets down a plate of Bredy with thick slabs of white, salty cheese. I pick at the corner of one piece of bread to be polite. I'm more interested in the coffee she brings on her next trip—it's purest black and as I swallow that first, bitter sip, the taste of it erases the smell of Jorge's house from the back of my throat.

Jorge's house always has this smell, the stench of mold and urine. I imagine the way your nose would wrinkle the moment you stepped through the door, Molly. You wouldn't think of stopping yourself.

I drink the coffee and in the background I hear you and your friends start to sing. "Jesus loves me this I know..." You sing in English.

"That's them," I tell Jorge and his mother. They look interested, but they can't understand the words you are singing. "For the Bible tells me so..."

"Oh, how pretty," Jorge's mother says. Then, "Teacher, do you like beef stew?"

"Ah, yes," I say, careful not to be too enthusiastic, because I don't want her to serve me any. Jorge's mother, she's like that. It's not what you're used to. No one makes it easy for you to say no.

"*VES*, Jorge?" she says, throwing up her arms. "Teacher likes beef stew! Listen, Teacher, I make beef stew for Jorge and he refuses to eat it. He says he doesn't like it. But it's good, right Teacher? Don't you see, Jorge?"

"At my house," I say, helping her to make her point, "it's nothing but rice and beans, rice and beans, rice and beans." I smile at Jorge. He scowls. He doesn't like me siding with his mother, so he'll punish me for it, give me the silent treatment for a while. As if that will upset me like it upsets other girls.

"SEE? JORGE?" Jorge's mother grunts loudly in annoyance, then mutters something to herself. She goes back to the stove to stir something. Beef stew, I presume.

Before I leave, Jorge stops scowling long enough to tell me he wants to meet you. He hasn't laid eyes on you yet, so it has nothing to do with your beauty; he's trying to piss me off, that's the only reason he requests this introduction. He thinks he can make me jealous. Jorge hasn't sensed my claustrophobia, the way I start to fidget when he suggests we go camp out in Jacó, just the two of us in a tent—he doesn't know that I'm glad he'll have you to distract him from me.

I bring him with me the next day to the church you're building. It's down the road from Cristián's house, at the very end, past the two new cement houses and the ten dilapidated shacks, the insides of which you will probably never see. Here's what's inside: living rooms, bedrooms, kitchens, bathrooms; families, chunches, photographs. Not so different from your house, and maybe even cleaner. Have you seen the way the women wax their floors? They are obsessed.

When Jorge sees you, he's impressed. You are prettier than I am. You know it, Molly. I'm not sad about that either; more catcalls for you, less for me. There is a balance in this town. Now you can be the beauty queen, and I'll just be the Teacher. For that, I am grateful.

I beckon. I introduce you to him and him to you, a Spanish accent on his name, an English one on yours. Jorge puts on his suave act. Then I leave the two of you together. I'm not about to hang around and translate for you, and besides, I think it will be interesting to see what happens when you try to communicate in your high school Spanish, which is atrocious, and Jorge's high school English, which is merely bad.

I turn to watch as I walk away and you seem to be doing just fine. Your chin is bending toward your shoulder already. He's staring at your hair. As yellow as the sun and twice as bright. Hard to look away from.

Forty minutes later you run to the house where I live, and instead of knocking you shout "*Upe*!" You've learned! I'm so proud of you Molly, that I feel the glow of pride come over me as I walk to the door. I feel like I do when one of my third graders picks up an English word I haven't taught yet, like when Andrés told me, "Teacher, I love you."

Anita's out of the house so we don't have to go through introductions, coffee, crackers, and polite chatter. I let you in and your smile is so big I notice for the first time how absolutely straight and small your teeth are.

"Oh my God, Oh my God, Oh my God," you say, the speed of your words reminding me how young you are: seventeen.

"Taking the Lord's name in vain?" I tease, but I'm actually surprised.

Your lips pucker. A dimple appears, deep in your cheek. "I'm not like that, Lana. I'm not all religious; I just wanted a vacation and my church was going to Costa Rica."

"And you heard it was beautiful?" You tell me yes, that's what you had heard. That's what people hear in the States, that Costa Rica is beautiful, and safe.

"So do you think it's beautiful here?" I ask, and you think for a second.

"Sort of." Your eyes wander; you pick up a piece of hair and begin to twirl it around a finger. "I guess it's not what I expected." I ask you what you mean, I'm truly curious. A year before, when I'd arrived, it hadn't been what I expected either. You say you expected the poverty and all, but why don't they try to make things just a little prettier? Like, why do they have to throw all their trash on the street? And would it kill them to paint their houses, so they're not all that same putty nothing color?

"Maybe they want to spend their money on something other than paint," I suggest, but to be honest, I've sometimes wondered the same things. A little color wouldn't hurt this town. And if I see a student throw a candy wrapper on the ground, I make the kid pick it up and put it in the trash can.

"Like food?" you ask, with pity in your eyes.

"No, like DVD players and coffee makers and washing machines." I think about explaining this further, but then consider the effort it will take, and so I go back to your subject. "So, you like Jorge?"

"He is so cute, Lana. He wants to take me to the Mirador in Juan Viñas."

Jorge used to take me there; he would drink ginger ale, I would drink Pilsen beer. "Are you going to go?"

"I'll have to see what Ursula says." Ursula is your monitor. You probably had to get permission from her to go as far as my house. She watches all of you, but mostly the girls, and especially you. She can smell it on you, Molly, just like I can. That dangerous curiosity. And that's why Ursula and I are looking out for you.

You might wonder, then. If I seem to dislike you so much, why would I want to look out for you?

I would like to address this question in your presence, but I can't. If you can look at me and think I am your friend, how can I explain to you that you are the enemy? How can you miss it, Molly—that look in my eyes when you say you feel sorry for the people here because they kill their own chickens? Your failed attempts at Spanish, and the way you roll your eyes, because you know you don't have to learn it? And the way you flaunt your money, Molly. It's simply obscene, taking cabs with your friends to the city, when you could take the bus like everyone else.

It's your church, your mission, your reason for being here, that bothers me more. You don't question the fact that your church bribes people into converting, actually pays them money. You don't see the irony when you come to my school, handing out bracelets and superballs and stickers that say "I love Jesus," in English, to the kids that don't know what that means, telling them they're gifts from God. That's how American you are—you express your faith materially.

I'm here to give you one last chance, Molly. You're young

enough for me to forgive you because I know you can change. I know you want more than what you were spoonfed. I see the way you look at the boys, the way you want to flirt with them. I know what you want from them, even if you don't. When I hear those hymns floating towards me in the schoolyard, your voice stands out, I hear it and I think: That's Molly. You are different from them, the ones who look at me with such shock when I tell them, "As far as I can see it, Jesus doesn't love me. Jesus doesn't even know me."

You're the only one who looks at me with eyes that sparkle.

But I can't just tell you this. If I am going to get you before you're gone, I can't just reach into the water and pull you out—you'll swim away. I have to bait you right, and I have to wait. This is all okay. I've learned, since I've been in Costa Rica, how to be very, very patient.

Your monitor won't let you go to the Mirador with Jorge, so I go with him instead. He sits over his ginger ale and sulks.

I sip at my Pilsen and say, "Don't worry, Jorge. We'll find a way."

He's taken off his school uniform and changed into jeans and a t-shirt. When I first met him, he lied to me and told me he was twenty. I wondered why he was still in high school, but a lot of kids repeat grades. I worried that he wasn't very smart. But his little sister is one of my students and she told me his real age: eighteen.

He dug his own hole with that one. You should never tell lies that are that easy to expose. Tico boys do it all the time, they lie without consequences. But Jorge learned a lesson; I told him that because he lied to me, I didn't trust him anymore.

"You know why I did it, Lana," he said, looking slightly outraged. "I knew you wouldn't go out with me if you knew I was only eighteen."

I told him, "I might have gone out with you if you were an eighteen-year-old who wasn't a LIAR."

They lie, Molly, even the good ones. They will lie to you and not even care if you know they are lying. The only way to punish them for this is to stand your ground.

I've stood my ground, but Jorge hasn't given up. He finishes his ginger ale, I finish my beer, and Jorge motions to the waiter for another round. He repeats for the tenth time today: "You know, Lana, that if you would be my girlfriend, I wouldn't be interested in Molly."

For the tenth time I say, "*Salado.*" If nothing else, Jorge's constant hounding gives me ample opportunity to use this, my favorite tico expression. *Too bad for you.* The other one I like is "*suave,*" which means stop or slow down. If you ever took the bus, you'd hear that, Molly, and you'd smile like me at the cleverness of such a small, solitary word.

Jorge shrugs. "I'll keep trying, Lana."

"Okay," I say. "Go ahead, Jorge; keep trying. I guess you're not too concerned about how that would look, La Teacher going out with a high school boy."

For a second he looks perturbed, and he says, "Lana, why are you talking *paja*. You're not that much older than I am, and anyway,

I like mature women." It's always about him, see.

"So why do you like Molly? She's younger than you are, Jorge. She acts even younger than she is."

Jorge smiles at me brazenly. "She has something. *Un toque*. I don't know what it is."

I promise Jorge that I will help him.

"What if you acted as her monitor?" he suggests. "Would Ursula trust you to look after Molly?"

"Maybe she would..." I touch my index finger to my forehead and press on my skull. Inside my skull, my brain is reeling. I'm reeling you in. "Maybe I could take her on a little day-trip," I suggest.

Jorge and I come up with a plan. We are going to take you to San José, Molly. We're going to get you there.

You've been outside the town before, of course. You've been to the places the gringos go. The butterfly farm. You walked on the plowed-over trails in the rain forest, screaming and giggling with your friends, scaring all the birds away. You got sunburned on the beach—on the Pacific side, of course; they would never take you to the Caribbean side, where those two gringas picked up the wrong hitchhiker and got themselves murdered.

You've been to San José already. You stayed in the Gran Hotel on Avenida Segunda, just steps away from the Plaza Central, where you and your Evangelical band gave your obligatory performance.

Here's what it looked like:

You walked to the center of the Plaza in a herd, looking suspiciously at the long-haired men around you. This is a target area for robberies. There are always so many gringos here.

You stood in a line with ten other girls. Behind you, the boys made up their own line. They always stand behind you, right? Yeah, right. You tried not to look bored as your minister picked up the microphone and began his speech. You'd heard it a million times.

"You are suffering," the gringo minister told the crowd. "Things are not always good in your life."

He handed the microphone to a tico man, some recent convert, who translated this. People stopped to listen. Yes, they thought. I suffer. They wanted to know how they could make that suffering stop.

You pulled at your skirt, it was hot outside, and the boys were beginning to sweat in their oxfords, making half-moon wet spots under their arms.

The minister told the crowd, "You feel a lack inside. This lack you feel is a hole. A God-shaped hole." The tico man stuttered, trying to translate this.

"GOD CAN FILL THE HOLE," the minister said. "LET GOD FILL THE HOLE."

Then you sang while one member of your group walked around and passed out pamphlets. You crossed your arms to better bear the weight of your bags full of souvenirs. The bags said, Café Rica. El Mall San Pedro. You came all the way to Costa Rica to go to the mall.

How do I know this? I see it every month. Days in San José when we happen to be around the Plaza, my friend Marissa and I sit on the steps and watch you, snickering and yelling things and cracking ourselves up. Lisa once stood up in the middle of a translation, looked behind the line of gringos, put her hands to her cheeks and yelled, "Look! Howler monkeys!," and those idiots turned around and looked. Another time, Anita had given me a napkin full of biscochos, fresh from the frying pan, as I'd left for San José. Lisa and I each took one, still greasy, and chucked them at the singing gringos. Lisa hit a tall boy on the arm. He looked around, his expression somewhere between scared and curious. I aimed mine, Molly, at a girl who could have been your twin. Her waist was small; her eyes were so blue I could see them from twenty meters away. She was comfortable in her skin in a way that only girls who look like you can be. She was giggling her way through the chorus of some song that I didn't know the words to because I was raised a heathen.

I aimed my biscocho at her head, but I was too far away. It hit her on the skirt, leaving a small grease mark near the hem. She shrieked and turned around, ran behind one of the boys, and grabbed his shoulders, using him as her shield. Everyone watched her as she gasped in air, wheezing through a laugh.

She was used to commanding attention. Even while she pretended to act scared, you could see how delighted she was, that everyone was looking at her. She did exactly what you would have done, Molly.

I didn't even know you yet. Yet I did.

I've known girls like you all my life. Summers I worked tickets and snack bar at Six Flags, and girls like you would come to my register and order Diet Cokes and nachos. They drove convertibles and there were always boys with them. When these boys were alone, they would come up to the counter, ask me for ice cream in coy tones. Sometimes I would agree to go on dates with them and they would take me to the movies, or to play mini-golf in the sweltering July heat. Sometimes we parked. I wouldn't have sex with them; there was only so much I was willing to risk. There was more than enough for me in fingers and tongues, in a boy's breath on my neck, and with certain boys, allowing them to bear witness to my pleasure was ample compensation for their efforts. But I got them off anyway. It was fair, and I liked being able to watch desire give way to satisfaction, how it registered, differently, real, on every boy's face.

I did this because I wanted to, but afterwards, some boys would look at me as if they'd gotten away with something. The next time they came into the snack bar they would pretend not to know me, or they would be with girls like you, and point at me and say something to them. The girls like you would glance at me, though they were usually polite enough to not stare too long. I wasn't hurt as much as I was perplexed.

I hated the way they giggled, these girls. I hated the way they wanted the boys around, but squirmed away from them when they were. I wanted to see one of them cry. I wanted evidence that just one of them was familiar with pain. Once, I did see one of them pink-eyed and weeping. A red-haired girl in a purple bikini ran into the snack bar, tears streaming down her face, and my heart swelled and dropped into my stomach. I had to know what had happened to her. I dropped my ice cream scoop into the cloudy water. She was looking around for someone to help her, it seemed, and I wanted it to be me.

But before I got to her, one of the lifeguards from the Louge next to the snack bar did. He swallowed a bite of his hot dog and took her by the arm.

She breathed in, seeming relieved. "I lost my tennis bracelet. It must have come off when I was going down the waterslide. It probably went down the drain!"

He was a hero, John, the lifeguard. He waded into the Louge landing pool, dodging kids coming off of slides, and their heavier, more dangerous parents, as they plunged into the pool. He could have gotten a foot in the face at ten miles an hour, but John dove, and when he finally climbed up the steps, he had a string of diamonds in his hand.

That girl had stopped crying the minute John took her arm. After this, I would watch him and the other male lifeguards do this over and over again, dive for lockets, for earrings, even for a cheap beaded friendship bracelet, to make a girl like that feel grateful. And when he handed her the bracelet, she hugged him, pressed her bare stomach against his, and went back to her friends, laughing, relieved that everything was in its place.

There were always the girls like you, Molly, and there were always the boys who liked them. I thought when we all got older things would change.

I came to Costa Rica to get away from people like you. I went as far away from you as I could get, and here you are.

*

You start coming over to my house every day, at my invitation. I don't let Jorge come over too often; I don't want to give Ursula anything to wonder or worry about. I serve you fresco from the fridge, made with boiled water and the store-bought mix that Anita gets from the super in Turrialba.

"I love this stuff," you say, swallowing it down.

"It's just sugar, chemicals, and food coloring," I tell you.

"Ew," you say, then you change your mind. "Well, who cares. I'll have some more." I never drink Anita's fresco, except when she offers it to me directly. I drink coffee, black.

I pour you more fresco. It's supposed to be the color of starfruit. It's as green as a crayon.

"So you're almost done with the church?" I ask, and you shrug and say "Yah." I ask you what's next.

"We're going on a river rafting trip, then we're going home," you say. "I have to start applying to college. My mom really wants me to go to Tulane. It's like her dream. But I think I'd rather go to UK." I pause for a moment, then realize you mean the University of Kentucky, and not the United Kingdom.

"Will you be sad to leave this town?" I ask.

"No," you laugh. "I haven't had a hot shower in two weeks. And Rudolfo won't leave me alone, he keeps coming by with ginger ale. I don't even like ginger ale. It looks like he peed into a plastic bag and stuck a straw in it. Ursula's beginning to get a little annoyed with him, too. And I'm really, really sick of rice and beans." You stop, suddenly seeming less sure of yourself. "Oh, but I loved meeting you, Lana. I'm so glad you were here. I don't know what I would have done if you hadn't been here."

"And Jorge?" I ask.

Your eyes roll back in your head. "He is so beautiful, Lana. He's the one reason, aside from you of course, that I wish I could stay here longer."

I'm priming you, Molly. I move from my spot on the stool and sit down next to you on the sofa. My thigh is touching yours.

"Tell me Molly," I say. "I know your church is opposed to premarital sex, but what would they have to say about good old-fashioned fooling around?"

You bat your eyes at me, as if to prove your innocence. "You mean like kissing and stuff?" I drum my fingers on my knee and smile.

"Cut the crap, Molly," I say. "You know what I mean."

"You can't tell anyone that I'm telling you this," you say. I realize I can feel my own pulse. You look over at the wall as if your history is being projected there. "The first time I ever fooled around with a guy was on a church retreat."

"A church retreat?" I repeat dumbly. I can't even imagine what that is.

"They're so clueless! They think that because we're so innocent and obedient they can put the girls and the boys right next to each other. What do they THINK will happen? The boys sneak into the girls' rooms, of course."

"The girls never sneak into the boys' rooms?" I ask.

You're biting the rim of your glass, now empty. You exhale

loudly through your nose and mouth and your breath fogs up the inside of the glass. How can your every action be so charming?

"No," you say. "The boys always come to us."

Just as you say this, I hear footsteps outside. Then Jorge's voice, a curt "*úpe.*"

I let him inside. He sits down on the couch and takes my place.

"*Voy a pasear*," I say, and leave, winking at Jorge. I cross the road, pick a rock, and sit on it, staring across at the house. I watch for Anita. She's playing bingo at the church—the real church. She shouldn't be back for a while but I keep my eye out just in case. Across the street, two of my students are playing in the gutter, poking sticks into the water. One of them spots me.

"Teacher!" he yells. It's Juan Carlos. He and his brother, Ernesto, shout out "Hello!" in unison, then go back to digging in the water. They're wearing those little rubber boots I love.

A tractor chugs up the road towards me, spilling sugar cane onto the road. There are sugary mud puddles on the road, and smashed cane everywhere. Flies hover over the bigger puddles. If you grab a piece of cane before it gets run over, you can suck the sweetness out of it.

The tractor passes. The three men sitting in the front seat turn to stare at me. The door opens with the tractor still moving, and one of the cane-cutters jumps out onto the road. He's wearing a t-shirt on his head and the same rubber boots that Juan Carlos and Ernesto wear. It's Gemelo, the father of five of my favorite students.

"Hola Teacher!" he calls as he approaches me. "What a beautiful day. It's like summer. No rain for days. True?"

Gemelo, and he slaps my arm a couple times. I kiss him on the cheek. "Come to the house sometime," he says, and I promise him that I will. I walk back across the street, avoiding puddles, tip-toe up to the door, and push it open.

Jorge's leaning against you with his hand up your shirt. You see me and start to giggle, pushing his hand away. Jorge looks at me. We lock eyes. He winks at me and then, I start to giggle too.

Three days before you're ready to leave, you and your friends come over to the school to play with the kids. As soon as I see you, I duck into the lunchroom. I sit on a stool meant for a seven-year-old and bite my nails for a while. The other teachers come in one by one. They drink fresco from a vat in the kitchen, dipping plastic blue cups into the sugary pool.

"Teacher, your friends are outside in the schoolyard," one of them says.

"They're not MY friends," I say, and the teachers explode with laughter. Lorena slaps me on the back.

"We're glad to hear you say that," says Lorena. "We were worried, them being your countrymen and all...but we'd really like to see them get the hell out of here."

"They're worse than Rogelio and Dorian," says Rosa, referring to two of the more zealous converts in the town. "At least Rogelio and Dorian only try to convert people by luring them into their homes, then talking the Bible to death. They don't try to seduce children with candy and toys."

"True," I say. His smile is huge; it always warms my heart. He kisses my cheek. Gemelo loves me and his love is platonic. He loves me because he knows I adore his kids.

"I see all your gringo friends are building a church down by Cristián's house," he says. "I see them around, but I can't talk to them, because I don't speak English!" He laughs. I wish he would say *because they don't speak Spanish*. "I tell Aida Carolina to talk to them in English, but she says she can't."

"We've only just started," I try to explain. "It took me ten years to learn Spanish. In ten years, Aida will talk like a gringa."

"They sang some songs," he says. "It's the work of God, Lana, all you gringos coming here to help our children."

Gemelo is *evangelico* too. Once I sat in his house as he made each of his kids recite the books of the Bible from Génesis to Apocalipsis. When the carnival came to the city nearby, his kids were not allowed to go. None of the *evangelicos* were. I asked Aida why she couldn't go, and she shrugged. I couldn't tell if she was sad or not.

I know why Gemelo converted; he told me the first day I met him. "I had vices, Teacher," he said that day. "I threw all my money away on liquor and cigarettes. Now that I'm with Christ, my money goes to my family."

That was the most common explanation I'd heard in this town from those who had converted. It was about family, and it was about money. But when people look at you, Molly, you and your friends, it's only about money.

I'd almost forgotten about you. "I'm going home," I say to

I tell them I agree, and Teresa brings me my own cup of fresco. I drink it. My body is used to the *bichos*; I won't get sick, like you would.

When I go back out to the schoolyard, I look for you among the gringos, but you're not there. The kids are decorated with new bracelets and half of them have little round stickers on their foreheads.

"They look like little Indians!" says one of your friends. I recognize him as the one who wears the shirt that says, "It's not a choice, It's a baby!"

"Here," I say, and hand him a fresh glass of fresco.

"Is it boiled?" he asks.

"Yah," I say, "drink it." And he does. People are so easy to boss around, Molly. It truly scares me sometimes.

You've been going around from door to door, passing out pamphlets. It's your last deed. The church is done and you're ready to leave town. After your rounds you stop by my house.

"Half the town was converted before we came," you say. "I spent most of the day drinking fresco while Father Andrew talked to them about the Bible. People are so nice here."

You show me the pamphlet. On the cover there's a picture of a blonde woman and her blond child. They're crouched next to a flowery bush, petting a bear. *A bear.* And there is a deer sipping from a lake in the background, and a couple holding hands next to a house, and a pair of birds fluttering by. The caption reads: "Life in a Joyful New World."

"Are you trying to tell me," I ask you, "that if we all became Christians, we could sit around petting bears?"

"I don't know," you say. I open the pamphlet and read it in Spanish. At the end of the pamphlet, after all the promises of happiness, there's a catch. Of course, there are requirements to be met if we are to live forever in the coming Paradise on earth. Does it list that you can't drink alcohol? Smoke? Dance at the *discomóvil*? Play Bingo? Wear spandex? Does it tell you to renounce your carnal ways?

Does it tell you that you have to give 10% of your salary to the church until you die? Because, Molly, these are the rules in this town. But it doesn't list them. It just says, Accept Jesus Christ as your Lord and Savior. That is the only requirement they tell you about now.

I look over at you. You're fanning yourself with a pamphlet.

"Do you really believe this stuff, Molly?" I ask you.

"Sure, some of it," you say. "Don't you think it would be such a beautiful planet, if only everyone could be nice?"

Anita walks through the door with a blue-and-white striped bag full of groceries. You still haven't met her. I open my mouth to introduce you, but you jump up and say "Hola," shake her hand limply, then turn your back on her.

"Gotta go," you say. "I'll ask Ursula if I can go to San José with you, I'm really excited, Lana." And you leave, smiling briefly at Anita on your way out the door. Anita stands there, looking confused. I apologize for you, Molly. I explain to her that customs are different in the States. It doesn't help explain to her why someone who came into her house, drank her fresco, and sat on her couch would flee the moment she arrived.

We eat mango to get your taste out of our mouths.

On the last day of your stay here, I am the one the kids come to, crumpled stationery in their hands, pencils poised. They ask me, "Teacher. How do you say in English, Dear Molly can you send me a gold bracelet, a poster of the Power Rangers, and a picture of yourself."

"Why are you asking her for these things?" I ask the first girl who came to me with this request. The first kid. I don't know if you know anything about kids, Molly, but once one of them does something, twenty more will follow.

"Because I ASKED Molly if she would send me these things. She said *sí, sí, sí*. I just want to make sure she doesn't forget."

"But Yeimi, Molly doesn't speak Spanish. If you asked her for these things, I doubt she understood you."

"Then why did she keep saying *sí, sí, sí*?" I'd like to know myself. But there is something else that you're leaving for me, Molly. Little Jenifer makes this known to me, just walks up to me while I'm eating my Chiki cookies during *recreo* and ruins my day.

"*Usted es una gringa*," she states, looking up at me, innocently. Yes, I say, I am a gringa. I think this is cute, and laugh a little. But then little Jenifer says, "*usted es turista*," and Molly, it's like I've been slapped in the face. She looks shocked that this doesn't win her the same pleased laugh that calling me a gringa had.

"A tourist?" I say. Frankly, I'm outraged. I'm outraged by the statement of a seven-year-old. "You think I'm a tourist? Jenifer, how long have I lived here?"

"Since last year," she shrugs.

"Why did you call me a tourist?" I ask.

"My *mamá* told me, gringos are tourists, and tourists are gringos," Jenifer says. I tell her that her mother is wrong. I give her a hug and half of my Chiki cookie but inside I boil and rage. Suddenly, I realize I might cry.

Look, Molly, what you have reduced me to.

I get up Saturday morning and pack my travel bag. A change of underwear, a shirt, my toothbrush and soap. The book I'm reading, my wallet, a notebook, two rollerball pens that my father sent me from the States. Then, Molly, something for you. Three Sheik condoms in a small, square box.

"Where are you going, Lana?" Anita asks me. I tell her San José. "Be careful of the *chapulines*," she warns. "Don't walk east of the post office." It's endearing, the way she always warns me of the same thing when I leave. The *chapulines* will never get me, Molly. I'm no *turista*, no stupid gringa. I tell her I'll be careful and she gives me a napkin full of biscochos for the road.

On the bus to San José I ask Jorge, "When you think of gringos, what do you think of?"

"You mean, do I like them?"

That's not what I meant, but now I'm curious. I ask, "Do you?"

"Yes," Jorge says. "I like some of them. But they're like everyone else in the world, Lana. Some gringos are good, and some aren't so good. It's like the Nicas. Everyone here in Costa Rica thinks that anyone who comes from Nicaragua is a thief or a murderer. Yes, some Nicas are thieves, but some of them aren't. All over the world. Good people and bad people. It doesn't matter where you are. Just because you're a gringo, it doesn't make you a God."

"That's why I like you, Jorge," I say. Then I think a minute and ask, "Do you think I think I'm a God?"

Jorge smiles and reaches for my hand. "No, Lana. That's why I like you." I let him squeeze my hand but then I pull it away.

Jorge continues, "People say things about gringos, there are the stereotypes. They say that all gringas wear loose clothes, but that's not true. Molly wears tight clothes." I don't bother to explain to him that most gringas think they're fat and feel no need to flaunt it. He wouldn't get this; no one does. The kids are always asking me if I'm pregnant because of my loose dresses. But girls like you don't have to worry about this. No worries, no worries, no worries at all.

It's noon when we get to San José. Jorge yells PARADA when we get to Parque Morazán and the bus pulls over to let us off.

You'll meet us here later, at the Turrialba/San José bus station. Ursula is letting you come because I promised her I'd meet you right at the station, and then drop you back at the Gran Hotel by eight o'clock. How predictable, Molly, that your clan is coming all the way back to San José, staying in a five star hotel, getting picked up by some fancy river rafting group, and climbing into a special van that will turn around and take you right back where you came from. The river runs straight through our town.

It was easier than I had imagined, getting Ursula to agree. All I had to do was bat my eyelashes, like you do. I made her think I was nicer, sweeter, and needier than I am. I told her, "Molly just has to see the ballet; she told me how much she likes to dance. And Ursula, it's been so long since I've had a friend. I'm all alone here, you know. Let me spend one last afternoon with Molly." I stuck out my lip. She pitied. She stopped just short of patting me on the head and said, "Okay, dear."

I want to do something nice for Jorge so I take him to the Gran Hotel for breakfast. We order pancakes. There's no syrup so I pour honey over mine. We watch the gringos sip at their genuine Costa Rican coffee.

"That's where the ballet is," Jorge says absently, pointing towards the Teatro Nacional, just across the plaza from the Gran Hotel.

"You know, this is where Molly and her friends are staying tonight," I tell him.

"Here?" Jorge's eyebrows rise. "They must be rich. How much does it cost to stay in a place like this?"

I tell him I don't know. I do, though. I read it in my guidebook. It's what I make in a month and a half.

"Well, the place I'm taking her, it's a little less pretty. But it's fine. You will see, Lana. It has everything you need." He smiles at me and I ask for the check. Jorge fights me for it, but in the end I pay.

This place, Molly, is like nothing I've ever seen. You'll pass right by it on the bus but you won't notice it; it's marked by a small blue sign with its name in block letters: HOTEL BRISTOL. Underneath it reads, "Open all night!" If it weren't for the sign there would be no way to know it was a hotel. It looks like any other hole in the wall. We get out of the cab, enter through the open doors, and walk up a few steps.

"How do you know about this place?" I ask Jorge.

"Been here before," he says, feigning nonchalance. He's told me how he had an affair with a married woman whose kids are my students. He won't tell me which woman, but he's given me enough details that I believe him. I want to know who it was, but I refuse to ask.

At the top of the steps is a closed gate. Beyond the gate, I see a room, but it's so dark that I can't tell what it looks like. I hear the TV going.

"*Upe*," says Jorge, and after a moment a teenage boy appears on the other side of the gate. He stares at us blandly and Jorge says, "I'd like to rent a room for a few hours." A few hours, Molly!

"How many hours?" asks the boy.

Jorge checks his watch and says, "I suppose six." He takes out his wallet and hands the boy two thousand-*colón* bills. The boy hands him a five-hundred in return and unlocks the gate for us.

We walk behind him into the lobby, which is completely dark except for the light coming from the TV, and the light coming from a fish tank in the corner. In the fish tank, there are two swollen goldfish, one black, the other gold.

"Take any room you like on the first floor," says the boy. "The ones on the second floor are all taken." He returns to his place in front of the TV. There's a soccer game on. "Do any of them have windows?" I ask. The boy tells me no. Jorge leads me into a room off the lobby that smells suspiciously like his house, though more of mold, and less of urine. There's a bed, of course, and a bathroom. A garbage can in the corner that has some garbage in it—a couple of balled up tissues, an empty packet of Deltas. The mattress is vinyl. When I sit down on it, the sheet pulls away, and I realize that the sheet has literally been thrown over the mattress, not tucked in. Why bother, I suppose.

"It's perfect," I tell Jorge. It's the seediest place I've ever been in. I'm electrified.

"Do you think Molly will like it?"

"Oh, yes," I say. I try to picture you sitting on the bed. Molly, if you want Jorge, I hope, I hope you'll take him. But it will be more likely that you won't. He'll have the condoms, and he has my blessing—but even without these things Jorge might feel he has a right to you. And I'm giving you a chance to take matters into your own hands; this is my gift to you. No one to hide behind, no one to give that cute pout to, Molly. Just you. Deciding what you want, and taking it.

Jorge sits down next to me on the bed. He sighs, pulls at his shirt. "It's hot in here," he says. He's not complaining; he's giving himself an excuse to remove his shirt. He pulls the t-shirt over his head and stretches out on the bed.

"You're hairy," I say, looking at his chest. I'd seen the hair poking up above the collar of his t-shirts from time to time, but I never imagined how ample it would be.

"As hairy as a monkey," he says, smiling. "Come here," he says, now pulling at me. He tugs at my arm, and I think, why not? I'll lie with him. I'm interested in how that chest hair will feel.

"I'll lie with you," I explain, "but that's it, Jorge. *De acuerdo*?" He nods, but he's only pretending to agree. Soon he's trying to kiss me. He's pulling my face so it lines up with his. His fingers make dents in my jaw.

"Jorge," I complain, breathing onto his face. "I told you. Cut it out." I inch further away from him, then lie still. Now he starts to beg, Molly, he begs like my students do when they want to color in their coloring books. "Ay Lana, porfa, porfa, please let me. I want to kiss you. Just a kiss. Porfa?"

This is all foreplay to Jorge. Girls here say no, even when they mean yes. They don't want to come off as sluts, see. "Quiet down, Jorge," I say, and then I stand up. "Okay. I've seen the room. We can go now. We have to meet Molly in an hour and it'll take us that long to walk."

I have to wait while Jorge pouts on the bed. Pouting can take a long time. I stand near the door, waiting, tapping my foot. I hear human noise coming from above us. Low hums. Monosyllabic male word-grunts. Above us, a couple is reaching their peak, and the walls are thinner than you might expect.

"Listen," Jorge says.

"In the middle of the day?" I ask.

"It's Saturday," Jorge says, as if I've missed something. "Listen," he says again, as the woman's voice grows louder, and louder, until she's almost screaming. Her voice is competing with the noise of the soccer game.

"Lucky her," I say.

"No," Jorge corrects me. "Lucky him."

It's always about him.

Jorge finally gets off the bed, heaves a sigh, and puts his shirt back on. He's doing his best to look depressed. "You know," he says, "that you're the perfect woman for me. The most perfect woman in the world."

How sweet, right Molly? *Right.* I smile in a way that I consider sarcastic and which he will interpret as flattered. I take two steps toward Jorge, put my hands on his shoulders, and kiss him on the mouth. When his mouth opens, I slide my tongue inside. He starts pulling at my hips and I close my mouth to end the kiss.

"One last thing," I say. I reach for my bag and fish out the box of condoms. He takes them from me and the look of lust on his face is replaced by an eagerness, a sense of purpose. God, they're *so* much like dogs.

Jorge tries to take my hand as we walk through San Pedro, but I keep it to myself. "I'm old enough to be your...teacher," I say, and we both laugh. We pass the mall. Teenagers hang off the balconies in spandex and extremely tight acid-washed jeans. Not your Evangelicals, Molly. We turn onto *calle* 14 and walk along in silence for a while. There is little traffic. I listen to the sounds our footsteps make on the sidewalk; Jorge's soft sneaker steps, my click-clocking sandals.

"Be good to Molly," I tell Jorge.

"I will," he says.

"I'm serious," I say. "Listen to her. Give her what she wants. Listen to her, Jorge."

We're crossing the street when Jorge suddenly grabs me by the sleeve. "Shit," he says in English. Of course. It was probably the first English word he learned. Jorge starts to run, towing me by my shirt.

"What's going on?" I ask, quickening my pace, but I won't go any faster than a speed-walk. I look around. There's a bunch of teenagers crossing the street behind us. Otherwise, there's no one around.

"Run," Jorge says. "RUN!"

"What are we running from?" I start to say. But then I realize that the teenagers behind us have started to run, too. They're running towards us. They're running after us.

"*Chapulines*!" Jorge lets go of me and starts to sprint. I run after him.

I'm panicked, Molly. I don't understand. These kids, they look like the kids at the mall. They're younger than Jorge, maybe younger than you. Half of them are girls. How could they be the *chapulines*?

I'm running as fast as I can in my sandals, jumping over potholes, looking for an escape route. Jorge keeps looking back to make sure I'm with him. I'm sure he could run faster, but he doesn't; he's looking out for me. He stays with me, Molly. He stays with me until they close in on us and one of the boys grabs me by the back of my shirt, almost knocking me down. He could have kept running, but he stopped.

"Let go of her," Jorge says, and I say "Get your fucking hands off of me." I struggle until I see that the boy has a knife in his hand. We're surrounded by twenty kids in fashionable jeans, cut-off shirts, and lipstick. A girl in a hot pink leotard stands in front of Jorge. She's got a knife, too.

"Here," Jorge says, and offers his wallet.

"Everything," the boy says, and we give him everything. My bag, my watch, and Jorge's leather belt. The girl in the hot pink leotard wants my earrings. I give them up. The boy with the knife goes through Jorge's pockets. When he finds the condoms, he holds them up, and they all start to cheer.

"You like to fuck the gringas, eh?" Those are his last words. He spits in my direction but misses; his saliva hits the street. The *chapulines* take off running. Jorge and I run the other way.

I cry, Molly. I hate myself for it, but I cry. I'm not upset about losing my things, except for the rollerball pens and the money. It's other stuff that bothers me. The things I should have known.

Jorge sits with me on the sidewalk. He's pissed, Molly—he loved that belt. And now he'll never have you. His chance is gone, and soon you will be too.

I push the tears off of my face and turn towards him. "I'm sorry," I tell him.

"Not your fault," he says.

"I didn't know that *chapulines* looked like that."

"What did you *think* they looked like?" he asks. I tell him I don't know, but I had my ideas. I thought they looked like the cane-cutters in town, once they'd taken the t-shirts off their heads and put down their machetes. I thought they were men in their twenties or thirties with dirt caught in their wrinkled skin. I thought they walked alone. I don't know why I thought any of this, other than the fact that those were always the people harassing me in the town, hissing *gringuita machita venga pa'ca.*

"I'm sorry it won't work out with Molly," I say.

"Well, we still have the room."

I look at him, confused. "But the condoms are gone, and we don't have any money to buy more. We can't exactly ask her to buy them."

Jorge shrugs. "It's not like I have anything to worry about. She told me she was a virgin." I watch him play with the laces on his sneakers. "People have sex without condoms," he explains. And right there, Molly. That's where it ends.

"Not you and Molly," I say. I say this in my Teacher voice and Jorge knows I'm serious. I get up and start to walk towards the Turrialba/San José bus station. We're late. You must be waiting. Jorge and I walk together in silence and while we walk I look at him and think, you just don't know who your enemies are. And your enemies are so often your friends, Molly. It will always be like this, I fear.

You're glad to see us. The Turrialba/San José bus station is not in a nice neighborhood; you were nervous to stand there all by yourself, no one but you and the ticket-seller. But nothing bad happened to you, Molly. Nothing bad has happened.

You give Jorge the money to take the bus back to town. He kisses you on the mouth, gently. You seem sad to see him go. I pull you away from the station, giving Jorge a nod. I'll see him tomorrow.

"How much cash do you have?" I ask you.

"About two hundred bucks," you say. "I haven't spent much since I've been here. There's not much to buy, except coffee."

You don't mind lending me some cash. You feel sorry for me. You ask me why I don't go to the police, and I explain, it happens all the time. It happens all the time. Nobody cares. We have the *chapulines* just like we have the rainy season and trash polluting the street.

"I just want to get to a phone so I can cancel my Mastercard," I say.

"What, you're afraid they're off charging things from the J Crew catalog?" You laugh, Molly, and you make me laugh, too.

"Then you can buy me dinner," I say.

I take you to the Thai place near the bus station, and cancel my Mastercard from the phone there. You eat your first Pad Thai and love it. We split lemony cheesecake for dessert. We order coffee. It's the first meal I've had in weeks that doesn't involve rice *or* beans.

"Where was Jorge going to take me, anyway?" you ask.

"To the ballet," I say, and you smile. Over lemony cheesecake, you and I are both innocent.

At the Gran Hotel you thank me for everything. "I learned so much from you," you say. You hand me two twenty-dollar bills, and your address written on a piece of stationery that one of the kids gave you as a gift. But I won't write you, Molly. I'm done taking care.

You look like you're waiting for me to hug you, your shoulders slumping slightly, as if you're afraid to make the first move. I take your chin in my hand. I kiss you on the lips, and you let me. For two long seconds our lips are pressed together. Then I make a loud smacking sound to let you know it's a joke.

"Okay," you say, laughing nervously.

"*Bueno*," I say. In your eyes I think I see questions I will never answer, but sometimes I only see what I want to see.

On Sunday morning, I'm back in the town, sitting on the grass in Marielos's yard, looking at the highway. I chew on stalks of cane with some of the kids that live in her house. There are about twelve of them in two rooms; I can't figure out if they are all brothers and sisters, or if some of them are cousins. Some of the girls are already composing letters that they want to send to you and your friends in the States.

I help them translate, knowing that you won't send them any

gold jewelry. You probably won't write them back. They're about to learn a lesson in disappointment. But that's what I'm here to do: teach.

Around ten o'clock, I see a sleek minivan come over the hill. It's one of those vans that only transports people like you and me—tourists and gringos, gringos and tourists. It's you, Molly, you and your friends.

"Look," I say to the kids, and point toward the van. As it passes I see Ursula in the front seat with the seatbelt pulled across her chest, and then I see you. You're waving. The little girls run to the edge of the highway, waving their arms, saying "*Adios*, Molly! *Adios*!" Their new plastic bracelets click on their wrists.

SIN ALLEY

Oscar could see that the entraceway was dark, but he shook the bars of the gate anyway. The doorman who had stood here the last time was not here now. "*Alo,*" Oscar said, and waited, and then he shook the bars again. He could see a boy asleep on a cot just inside the gate. It was three a.m., it was one of San José's worst neighborhoods, and it had been a long walk to get there. Oscar had no intention of walking back to the centro until he knew if Martín was inside. "*Alo,*" Oscar said again, and finally the boy pushed the sheet off his legs and padded barefoot to the gate, grinding at his eye sockets. "Is Martín home?" Oscar asked.

"I don't think so, but come on in if you want to so badly." The boy opened the gate for Oscar, gave him a little shove to get his slow feet clear of the door, and climbed back into the cot and curled up against the wall. Even those ten-year-old *cacheros* knew how to push Oscar around.

Oscar had been shuffling, slow to enter, it was true. He knew there was a reason to watch his step. He instinctively covered his nose and mouth with his hand, and breathed through his teeth as he looked down. There it was, just like last time: a minefield of dog feces leading all the way into the house. When he'd come here with Martín, Martín had ushered him into the first room off the hall without mentioning anything about the dogs that must have been under house arrest, and by the time they'd gotten into the room Oscar quickly became preoccupied with the sight of Martín undoing his belt and his own nerves and forgot to pursue it.

"What *is* this?" Oscar asked through his hand.

"Welcome to Sin Alley," said the boy, and pulled the sheet over his head. In the gesture of rejection he exposed his feet, which flopped like fish surrendering on the bug-eaten foam rubber mattress.

"I mean the shit."

"Cinderella says, 'No police officer would risk getting involved with this much shit.'" The boy's feet disappeared under the sheet.

"He's right about that," Oscar said, and started down the hall.

"Who's in charge of walking the dogs?" Oscar asked.

Lorenzo's long eyelashes did bat, but to Oscar it did not seem deliberate, just the involuntary actions of a pretty boy. "They're Cinderella's. No one messes with them. But I have been known to mop up after them."

Two large black dogs of an ambiguous breed lay on the kitchen floor. Oscar could hear at least one other scratching against a door that lead to the kitchen. That door had a chain on it.

"There are two other dogs inside that room, they haven't been out in two years," Lorenzo told Oscar. "And I don't mean out of the house. I mean out of that room." Lorenzo said this with a know-it-all smirk.

"Cinderella keeps them in there? Why?" Oscar was horrified.

"I think they're guarding his things."

Lorenzo was eating gallo pinto with a big spoon and taking drags off a joint between bites. Lorenzo was blond-haired and fair, but the way he ate—hunched over, speaking with his mouth full—repelled Oscar, despite the kid's good looks. Oscar busied himself by checking the soles of his sneakers, then, since he was down there, he rolled up the cuffs of his jeans for the sake of something to do. A mouse skittered along the kitchen counter, followed closely by another.

"This place is truly filthy," Oscar said.

Lorenzo laughed, shooting a few grains of rice out of his mouth. "You think?"

"Why doesn't someone clean it up?"

Lorenzo picked up the last bean from his plate and flicked it towards the counter top, where the mice had passed. "Listen, *mae*, I'll give you some advice. If you're going to be hanging around here, you'd better not say anything about the dogs or how dirty it is or anything else in front of Cinderella, because Cinderella will ream you. I've seen him do it before. So watch yourself."

"Thanks for the advice," Oscar said. He wasn't scared. This kid was like fourteen.

"He'll turn you into a mouse. He's a witch, you know. Those mice are probably old clients who pissed Cinderella off."

"Of course," said Oscar wearily.

"Why don't you go into the salon? There are guys in there if that's what you want. What are you doing in the kitchen, anyway?"

"I'm waiting for Martín."

"I told you, he might not come in tonight. If you want a handjob, I can do it. I only do handjobs though."

Oscar thought about it. "How much?"

"Just five thousand. I'm cheap but I'm good."

"A toucan for a massage! Do you think I'm an idiot?"

Lorenzo shrugged. "You have nice shoes, and you look nervous. And I am very good."

"It's not my first time," Oscar said, "And I worked very hard to pay for these shoes."

Lorenzo rolled his eyes. "Three thousand."

The metal gate out front was silent. Oscar looked towards the hallway anyway, but it was empty. "One thousand," he told Lorenzo.

"Cinderella takes one thousand just for the room," Lorenzo said. Oscar went up to two thousand, and Lorenzo snatched up his plastic plate and tossed it in the sink.

"Just wash your hands first," Oscar said.

Lorenzo led Oscar through the living room, where other boys sat on flimsy crushed velvet couches, looking at the television and holding bottles of Imperial over their crotches in obscene postures. The volume was turned down low, but Oscar could hear the drowned moans of a woman as she performed oral sex on a man who was an actor in a movie but who was actually receiving oral sex all the same.

"Is it better to give or to receive?" Oscar's mother had often quizzed him when she was alive. Usually before giving him something he did not need but coveted deeply—a new soccer ball, a frozen *boli* to slurp on, or a twenty-*colón* coin for a snack during school.

And Oscar replied, "To give, to give, to give!," and meant it.

Oscar's mouth was the sweet wet gift to be put in the palm of Martín's hand, around his member, over his eyelids and under his whiskerless chin. Oscar would greedily hand over the money he'd made sloshing around in beer troughs for the permission to make this offering. To give!

The boys in the salon didn't appear to register Oscar's presence, nor did they seem alerted to his potential for generosity. They looked too settled in, considering where they were, staring at the screen with fish-like eyes. Most of them wore jeans and t-shirts, though one looked like he walked straight out of the Duckhead store in the San Pedro Mall, all starched and ironed. There were crumpled cigarette packets on the pocked coffee table, and so many Imperial beer bottles to varying degrees of emptiness (or fullness, depending on how you looked at it) that someone could probably line them up and play a little tune on them with a spoon. The boys' mouths had fallen into the marginal frown of boredom. Oscar didn't get a second glance as he followed Lorenzo into the empty room off the salon. If Oscar had walked into the salon alone, they would have livened up a bit, hoping to be picked up themselves. Knowing that didn't make him feel much better about being ignored.

The unoccupied room was lit by a lightbulb dangling on a

wire. There was a stove that looked like it had never been used, unattached and shoved against the wall like a regular piece of furniture. Someone had placed a board over the stovetop and on top of that, a bottle of lotion, a condom, a roll of toilet paper, and a bottle of Sanipine. There was the overwhelming disinfectant smell of Sanipine braided with the sharp grassy semen smell, and Oscar concentrated hard on not looking at the sheet as he sat down on it. When he looked up, he was confronted with a faded image of Britney Spears squeezed into a red latex bodysuit.

Lorenzo picked up the bottle of lotion without ceremony, squeezed it, rubbed the lotion between his hands to make it warm, and perched next to Oscar, who closed his eyes as Lorenzo's hand wrapped around him. Oscar tried to remember Martín's face, but things got fuzzy. Then he stopped thinking. As soon as he came, though, there was Martín's face again, right where it had been all week, on the backs of his eyelids.

A tear of suffering, triggered by that other release, filled each eye. Lorenzo was wiping his hands with toilet paper.

"What are you crying about, you sissy faggot?" he laughed at Oscar. "Don't tell me you didn't enjoy that." Lorenzo shot the baseball-sized wad of toilet paper across the room and made the shot, though Oscar had noticed earlier there was more toilet paper around the trashcan than in it.

"Yes," Oscar said. "I did enjoy it." That was a lie he told to avoid hurting Lorenzo's feelings. He tucked his shirt into his jeans and paid the boy. He went out through the living room, his head down, and hopscotched through the corridor, wanting out. The doorman had returned to his post, and he held the gate open for Oscar, and the sleeping boy rolled over, disturbed by the click of the gate.

"Until tomorrow," Oscar said to the doorman, trying to make a joke out of his situation. The doorman smiled perfunctorily.

Oscar had never solicited sex on the street, and had no intention to do so the night he met Martín. It was two in the morning and Oscar had just finished his shift at the Bar Burbujas, a somewhat upscale bar where he poured drinks and washed glasses and served *bocas* of fried tortilla and ceviche in order to pay for his tuition at the University. He was studying tourism, and had landed the job at Burbujas because his English was decent, though even the gringos who came into Burbujas hardly taxed his vocabulary. They said little to him beyond "Imperial, *por favor*," though once in a while he'd get a young gringo hell-bent on learning Spanish who seemed eager to talk to anyone who'd respond. Oscar held up his end of the conversation with these gringos in English while they spoke Spanish, which helped him learn some, but his English was sloppy; he needed the discipline of grammar texts and tense drills. But by the time he picked up Martín in Parque Morazán, he hadn't been going to classes for three months. He had stopped going to University when his sister Vivi found herself pregnant again and needed help. He'd picked up a few extra shifts at the bar.

Vivi had waited a long time to be pregnant again. Her first

child, Marielos, was now twelve, and she seemed to be the only soul God would give up for Vivi, which depressed her no end. Twelve years later, God came through. Vivi had been so desperate for her husband's Y chromosome to meet up with her X that she couldn't wait out the last months just to find that her hopes had been dashed, and went to the Clínica Bíblica complaining of stomach pains so they would give her an ultrasound.

It was not a public hospital and it was not cheap, but Vivi was given an ultrasound, and the ultrasound did show the little rice-grain of a penis, or whatever it looked like. Oscar couldn't imagine. Vivi, relieved, thought a son would bait her husband back into the house, full-time.

"Juan Carlos is God knows where," Vivi, seven months pregnant, said. "He takes his truck to Limón and I don't see him for days. He says he doesn't have to go anywhere until Tuesday, and then Sunday morning I wake up and he's gone and so is the truck! Shouldn't he just leave me altogether if he's going to be such a son of a whore?"

"Do you want me to come there?"

"Yes," she'd said, "And bring some eggs and coffee. He didn't even leave me a *rojo* to buy food with."

Vivi asked for food rather than money, but Oscar gave her money anyway. She was his sister. And little Marielos, who wound up doing at least half of the housework, she'd certainly earned some treats. If Oscar didn't help them, who would? It wasn't a lot of money but say something happened and Juan Carlos wasn't around for the next trip to the clinic?

But so far nothing had happened except trips to the super for rice and beans, lard and Sanipine, batteries for Marielos' CD player, cherry-flavored gelatin to make Vivi's fingernails stronger and prevent split ends. And so when he met Martín in the Parque Morazán, he had some money to burn.

Choosing to forgo his habitual route through Parque España, and pass, instead, through the tall-treed Parque Morazán, where all sorts of bad things were known to happen at this hour of the night; knowing that, especially because his shoes were nice, he might be the one to feel the knife-edge pressing cold into his throat, Oscar felt the strangest sensation: a total lack of fear. He had avoided this park for years because he was afraid of the people in it, but walking across it as he was now, going inside, he was now one of those people, implicated. And the lack of fear surprised him and was not entirely comforting.

Martín was standing under a tree with his hand behind his back, slick-haired, green-eyed, waiting, watching Oscar walk towards him, and Oscar saw him look down and notice his shoes before his gaze returned to Oscar's face. But who was afraid? What was Oscar afraid of losing, then, his money? This guy was so beautiful, and so tragic for whatever brought him to this park, that Oscar would gladly have handed him the burning wad had the stranger asked for it.

Instead, he was being offered something for it. "Do you want to go somewhere?"

Oscar didn't bother to bargain, afraid that a tactical mistake would betray his naïveté, and agreed to Martín's price of five thousand colones.

"My apartment's a busride away," he told Martín. This was a lie that Oscar told out of fear. His heart beat under his Adam's apple and his palms were so shiny they looked doll-plastic.

"I know a place," Martín said. He put his hands in the pockets of his jeans and led Oscar south through San José, walking slightly ahead of Oscar, though Oscar did try to keep up.

"Where is it that we're going?" Oscar asked.

"Just a place I've been crashing for a few weeks," Martín replied without turning his head. They passed through the Plaza de Cultura, where Oscar noticed several other boys about Martín's age, sixteen or so, standing alone, or sitting on curbs and steps, waiting.

"Where were you born, San José?"

This time Martín did look at Oscar. "Look," he said, "I'd prefer not to talk."

"Okay," said Oscar, but he was hurt. Then he remembered he was in a position to demand things.

"What am I paying you a toucan for if you can't meet such a simple request, for conversation?"

Martin looked sideways at him—weary, condescending—and sighed. "All you *playos* want is to talk, talk, talk, be told you've got a nice ass, well, you can forget it. I'm going to let you blow me because you're paying me. And you'd better be good."

The last comment, combined with the derogatory *playo*, confused Oscar, but at least he was pretty confident in his oral skill.

"At least tell me where you're from," Oscar said.

"San José. Now *callate.*"

Oscar did shut up, relieved to hear that Martín was not from Cartago. He wanted to know how long Martín had been prostituting himself, but wondering about that led to speculation about how many men he might have slept with, which made Oscar worry about HIV, so he stopped thinking about that. For some reason, it was his niece Marielos whose image emerged to fill the vacated space in his thoughts. Recently Marielos had cut her waist-long hair into a feathered bob that fell just below her chin, and the haircut seemed to have changed Marielos' personality completely. Even her smile had changed. She used to show joy with all her teeth, and her *china* eyes closed into little slits; now she smiled with her mouth closed, which created a puckered dimple in her right cheek that Oscar had never noticed before. Something was going on with Marielos. The hardness in her body and the softness in her soul seemed to be trading places. And Oscar did not like it. He missed the sweet, small Marielos who would jump into his arms.

Martín led him down the street where all the Chinese restaurants stood shoulder to shoulder, their grates down for now. Across the metal slats of Dynasty, someone had spraypainted in red, "*Chinos* eat mice," and someone else had tried to cross it out in black. One block further south, Martín stopped in front of a door marked with an exhuast-smudged plaque, and a man dressed in a black t-shirt opened the door for them. Oscar held his breath.

Kneeling in front of Martín, Oscar held his hands in the air, and they shook.

"Do you like it?" Martín taunted, holding his penis, which was rather impressive to Oscar.

"Please let me touch it," Oscar said.

"You'll have to beg some more, *reina*."

"Please, please, permit me."

Martín was leaning back on the bed. He reached down and took his t-shirt by the frayed bottom and pulled it over his chest, revealing a hairless, boyish chest, and purple nipples.

"Do you want to touch my skin?"

"Yes, please, let me touch you."

"You can't touch me anywhere except you know where with your mouth," Martín said, and the minute Oscar took him, with his trembling empty hands, that's when Oscar was hooked.

After his encounter with Lorenzo, Oscar couldn't shake the feeling of lard grease on his skin, the image of Lorenzo with his mouth full of gray, half-masticated gallo pinto (specks of which had landed awfully close to Oscar's arm on the table as Lorenzo spoke), and the awareness of the urine that must have been on his shoes. Several times on the way back to his apartment he lifted up his feet to recheck his soles, even stopping once to take off his right shoe and sniff it, which was a mistake. He left his shoes on the welcome mat and went straight to the shower.

The filth of Cinderella's house had gotten him thinking about his mother. She would have been mortified by the many ways Cinderella's house defied the laws of cleanliness. Certainly she had never imagined anything like that house. "Imagínate," Oscar said to himself, shuddering under the cold water stream, working a new bar of Bactex into a violent lather. Not that his mother had been that kind of a fanatic in practice, only in theory. She mopped; she cleaned the toilet and shower with Sanipine, like any other woman, but it was more what she knew about cleanliness that frightened Oscar enough to run under the cold-water stream each childhood morning.

As a child Oscar had been afraid of cockroaches because he once picked one up as it crawled across his bedroom floor, and his mother smacked his hand so hard that the critter flew across the room and wound up behind his bed, where, in Oscar's mind, it stayed, tormenting him for months. "You're unclean now!" his mother said, more afraid than angry. "Go wash in the *pila*!" That seemed to be a moment of insanity on Oscar's mother's part, since there were cockroaches everywhere in Costa Rica, and no one had a problem stepping on them, though it sometimes seemed superfluous. After that outburst, though, fear rode on the backs of the roaches. He was afraid, also, of Jorge, a Cartago kid who had flaky, red skin on his arms and neck, because his mother told him, "In Biblical times, that child would have had to have announced himself, 'Unclean! Unclean!' every time he walked through town." Of course, all sexual acts rendered one unclean, which Oscar knew very well without his mother having to tell him. Especially the ones Oscar thought about.

Oscar's mother considered herself a devout Christian scholar. She sought out Jews and talked to them about their faith, read the Old Testament and marveled at such an insecure God—the one she feared the most; she knew how quickly insecurity gave way to wrath—then reread the New Testament until she could settle back into the comfort of forgiveness. She made the pilgrimage to the church in Cartago every year, but since she already lived in Cartago, it wouldn't have been much of a sacrifice to do it from home, so she took the bus to Turrialba and walked all the way back barefoot, her shoes in her hand.

She was very overweight and it was always quite hot, and by the time she reached the church, the soles of her feet were bloody from scuffing the pavement.

Oscar and Vivi's mother dropped dead while hanging the clothes on the barbed wire fence behind the house. She was alone when she died. Oscar had just moved into his own apartment in San José, and Vivi was already married to Juan Carlos. When their mother fell, she was holding one of her giantess-sized bras by the strap, a plastic clothespin not far from her other hand where it lay on the ground. Ana Yanci from next door found her clutching the stretched-out elastic, lying face-down in the dirt. It would have upset his mother to know that she would be found this way, grasping at her intimate apparel. But at least she died before finding out her son was gay.

Most uncleanliness was removed simply by bathing. Oscar soaped himself from head to toe with Bactex and missed his mother badly. He'd shared a bed with her until he was seven, Vivi in the bed next to them, resentful. Nights, sometimes, he'd cry against his mother's softness, wanting to tell her something, but not knowing what it was. "Hush, *mi amorcito,*" she would say. "There's nothing to be sad about," she said, stroking his hair. He cried hot tears in the shower, thinking of her. When he washed his penis, though, he had to think of something else, especially because he spent more time soaping up this body part than any other, and so he thought of Martín, and was hard again.

"Don't cry for me Costa Rica…*coño* I wish I could leave you..."

Cinderella sang bitterly as he made his way to the gate, where Oscar waited. He emerged from the kitchen wearing a cheap satin bathrobe that had an accidental fringe of loose threads along the bottom, walking like a queen down the hall, which, to Oscar's great relief, had been mopped. He was followed by two dogs.

"I'm busy cooking, but please come in and make yourself comfortable in the salon," Cinderella said, opening the gate.

"I was hoping to see Martín."

Cinderella pursed his lips, and the skin sunk in below his cheekbones dramatically. Oscar could see that Cinderella had been stunningly beautiful in his youth, pretty like a girl. "Martín's in the pool hall next door. I hate to go outside because of the neighbors, they all hate me. They're all afraid of me, of course, but they still say nasty things. Would you like me to call him?"

"Well, I can wait here for a while." Oscar knew that he could go over to the pool hall himself, but he hoped to get Cinderella to tell him a little about Martín. "May I join you in the kitchen?"

"Yes, come have some coffee," Cinderella said over his

shoulder. Behind him, one of the dogs lifted its leg and peed on an ornamental plant.

Cinderella stirred rice and beans in a wok on a two-burner hotplate. "You're the sexiest man we've had around here in days," Cinderella said. "Why don't you let them fight over you in the salon? There are five hot boys in there."

"I'd like to wait for Martín," Oscar said. Cinderella pushed the gallo pinto around with a spatula, and seemed to have forgotten about the coffee, which was just as well. Oscar didn't even want to know what the inside of the coffee maker looked like. "Can you tell me anything about Martín?"

"Well, he's just like all the other boys around here, completely ungrateful, gorgeous, with a nice big dick. Look at this, here I am, slaving away over the stove, spending all my money on them, and do you think one of them will thank me for giving them a hot meal when no one else will? These boys have sucked me dry. At least Lorenzo mopped the hall for me today."

"Does Martín live here?"

"With his girlfriend, until she gets herself pregnant, and then they're out."

"His girlfriend?" Oscar was surprised, more for the fact that a woman lived in such a house than at Martín having a girlfriend.

Cinderella gave Oscar a pitying smile. "Yes, *cariño*. His girlfriend. All of these *cachero*s have girlfriends to prove they're so macho, and then they have to have eleven kids. They don't even know how gay they are." Cinderella turned off the hotplate and left the pinto sizzling in the wok. "They can come get their own food when they're hungry, the bastards, I'm not going to be their *mami* today."

It was two-thirty in the afternoon, and Oscar's shift started at four. "Maybe I'll go try the pool hall to see if he's there," Oscar said.

"Do that. And I'm going back to bed," Cinderella said.

"Can I ask you another question?"

"Of course, *cariño.*"

"Why do they call you Cinderella?"

Cinderella smiled wearily and said, "It's a long story for another time." He padded down the hall towards the room where Oscar had been with Martín.

Lorenzo whispered something to Julio. Julio was even younger than Lorenzo, maybe twelve. The contrast between the two boys went beyond the fact that Lorenzo was pale and blond and Julio was blackberry-dark; Lorenzo looked healthy, had all his teeth, and his teeth were white; Julio had a small scar above his eyebrow, was reticent, and his eyes had a yellow glow. Julio looked like a poor kid from the campo, and Lorenzo had the confidence of a city child.

"We think he's a witch," Julio told Oscar.

"He says he is, anyway, and he has this altar in the salon," Lorenzo said.

Oscar had been too preoccupied to notice any altar when he was in the salon. "So what's the story with his name? Cinderella's not a very good name for a witch."

Lorenzo held his hand up to Julio, who had opened his mouth to begin the story. "I'll tell it," Lorenzo said. "His mother was a whore in Alajuela. She had twelve children by twelve different men. She abandoned them all except Cinderella."

"She sold Cinderella," Julio put in.

Lorenzo nodded. "She sold him to a rich *tipo* who worked in San José and was never home and his stepmother was wicked."

"She didn't let him play at all, not even soccer," added Julio.

"Which probably is the reason he turned into a fag. She didn't believe in playing, and made him clean the house all day long."

An older boy, around Oscar's age, entered the kitchen and made himself a plate of pinto, and headed back towards the salon.

"But the stepmother had a daughter, and she loved her, but she didn't love Cinderella."

"So she bought Cinderella to do the housework," Oscar said.

"No, they had servants for the housework," Lorenzo said. "She just didn't believe people should be lazy. That's what Cinderella says. One day, the daughter wanted Cinderella to make her pancakes for breakfast, and it was Sunday, and Cinderella wanted to go to the Evangelical service at the crazy lady's house. The daughter told him he couldn't go to some *loca*'s house and grabbed his hand and dragged him all the way across the room. So Cinderella pushes her into the wall and says, Let me go or I'll break your little chicken neck. And the daughter went running to her mother and she came out and said, Listen, you little piece of street trash, you're the son of a whore, and by the way, get out of my house."

The older one had not gone back into the salon after all. He stood in the doorway of the kitchen, leaning his hip against the doorframe.

"That's when Cinderella started living on the streets." The boy was a man, with a deep, grave voice. "And he lived on the streets for five years. Which is also why he spends every last *colón* on these boys, so they won't have to live on the streets like he did, eating ugly bread out of a garbage can. Right, Lorenzo?"

"Right," said Lorenzo. He looked down at his rice and beans, but then looked up at Oscar and smiled. It wasn't a totally jaded smile, either.

"When you're done, you should go back into the salon," he said to the boys, and the dogs followed him in the direction of the room where Cinderella had gone to sleep.

"Cinderella is a stinky queen, but he is like our mother," Julio said.

"I hate the idea of boys as young as you in a place like this," Oscar said, though even saying it gave him a secret thrill.

"I only do handjobs," said Lorenzo.

"I just let them blow me," said Julio. "That's all the old men want. I go with the *viejos*."

"The *viejos* are the best to go with," Lorenzo agreed. It was dawning on Oscar that they were no longer looking at him as a client; Lorenzo hadn't seemed to even in the beginning.

"Well, if you don't get out of here soon, you'll be taking it up the ass," Oscar said.

Neither of the boys looked scared. "No way," said Lorenzo. "I'm out of here any day now. And even if I stayed, I would never do that."

"You're a liar," Julio said. "I saw you go with the Russian, and tht's all he comes here for."

"No I didn't," Lorenzo said.

"Yes he did," Julio said to Oscar.

Lorenzo rolled his eyes. "You've been on the other side of a blowjob once or twice yourself."

"No I haven't."

Oscar covered his mouth with his hand, trying not to laugh.

Lorenzo's mood had turned. "Why are you always sitting here in the kitchen?" he demanded of Oscar. "Are you one of those religious people who comes here to lecture us about how we shouldn't be doing this, and then asks us how much?"

"No, I'm just waiting for Martín."

"Martín? He's in the salon," Julio said, and Oscar felt the sweat fill up the lines of his palms.

"If you want another handjob sometime, I'll lower my price for you," Lorenzo said to Oscar, blinking his long eyelashes, not winking, and began to clear the table.

No matter what anyone had said, did say, would say, Martín was a beauty, and when you believed in beauty as much as Oscar did, you could not help associating it with goodness. Martín was smoking what looked like a *basuko*, or else it was just plain pot, laughing with another *cachero* in the salon. His legs were splayed, his jeans tight, and he was wearing a white ribbed tank top that had a small yellow stain in the area of his heart. No—Oscar was wrong. The heart was on the other side. That was good; Oscar didn't appreciate obvious signs.

"I remember you," Martín said, smiling coyly at Oscar and nearly sending him swooning into the doorframe.

"Can we?" Oscar pointed at the room where Lorenzo had taken him earlier. Above them, the sky opened up all at once, and the rain filled the house with its noise, which reminded Oscar to look at his watch. It was 3:15; he was going to be late to Burbujas.

The other *cachero* picked up the remote control and a soccer game appeared on the television screen. Martín walked ahead of Oscar into the room, stepping over a pile of dog shit that sat on the floor in front of the unattached stove.

"Ay!" Oscar took a step back. "This is ridiculous! Those dogs shit in every corner of the house!"

"A dog's got to do what a dog's got to do." Martín lay down on the bed and pulled his shirt up to expose his smooth, brown stomach. "Do you want the same deal for five thousand?"

"I want the same thing but I want you to touch me, too."

"Six thousand."

"I only have five." This was a lie Oscar told because he did need the other thousand for bus fare, and to pay for his dinner.

"I'm giving you a break, but don't ask for anything extra," Martín said.

"Please let me kiss you on the mouth," Oscar whispered.

"You can't kiss me anywhere," Martín said, shock-serious. "If you try, you will truly regret it."

"Martín, you shouldn't stay in this place, it's disgusting."

"I don't notice." Martín's green eyes were glazed. "Do you want to touch me?" he asked.

Oscar did. "Beg," Martín said, and Oscar begged.

Marielos, Oscar's niece, had never been a very attractive girl in Oscar's eyes, though he loved her. Her skin was dark in that way that looked charred, and her eyes were too *chinita*. Now, at twelve, the trunk of her body had become perfectly rectangular; the two little pyramids of her budding breasts didn't seem to belong there. Oscar could tell she was going to be fat someday.

Vivi was fat already. Lipid-filled pockets of skin folded over her knees. She'd grown a second chin and was working on a third. It was in the genes. Vivi and Oscar's mother had weighed over one hundred kilos when she finally tipped over and died while hanging the clothes.

"She ate too much grease," the doctor told them later. "All her little tubes were clogged with it."

Oscar had stopped putting lard in his food. He learned to add oil, instead, to his rice when he cooked it, and he fried his onions and peppers in Salsa de Lizano.

Old habits died hard with Vivi. Oscar watched her scoop a whopping dollop of lard into the gallo pinto as she stirred it in the frying pan. Gallo pinto was made from last night's rice and beans, and Oscar was fairly certain that she'd put in plenty of lard last night, too.

"I'd like some cereal," Oscar said. He picked an ant out of the sugar bowl before scooping sugar into his coffee.

"Marielos!" Vivi shouted, though Marielos was sitting not two meters away from her, writing something in her school notebook.

The notebook was covered in plastic and made a crinkling sound under the pressure of Marielos' ballpoint. Marielos bent further over her work to finish whatever she was writing, then stood up to go to her mother. Marielos had once shot forward like a housedog when she was called. Now, she stood, balanced her weight on her feet, and walked with her hips jutting from side to side, her litheness lost.

This Marielos seemed to bear no relation whatsoever to the Marielos he'd known for eleven years. Oscar couldn't make sense of it; it wasn't as if she'd become a woman in all of six months. She was simply another person altogether.

Marielos stood beside her mother, waiting for instructions with her hand on her hip. It was a gesture just this side of mockery.

"Get some money out of my purse and go down to the *pulpería* and get your uncle Oscar some cereal."

Instead of taking money out, Marielos slung her mother's purse over her shoulder and went out through the open door.

Oscar took a bitter sip of his coffee. "Wait," he called, and Marielos stopped in the yard. The sun reflected off her black hair so that the crown of her head shone white. "I'll accompany you." He took a minute to finish his cup. Marielos stood in front of a chayote vine, waiting for him, tapping her foot. To Vivi he said, "Don't worry, I will pay for the cereal. Cereal is very expensive."

"Get me some soda crackers, too, and cream cheese," Vivi said.

Oscar and Marielos walked down the dirt road together, silently at first. Marielos had a smile on her face for a reason Oscar couldn't fathom.

"Uncle Oscar, I want to tell you something."

"What's that, *China*?"

"I have a boyfriend."

"No, don't tell me!" Oscar grabbed her around the shoulders, which Marielos seemed to like. Her body became limp in his hands; there was a receptive feeling to her sudden limberness. Then Oscar thought of something. "Tell me about him. How old is he?"

"Twenty." Marielos was smiling so hard it hurt to look at her. Oscar was twenty-three. He did not smile. He took her firmly by the arm.

"Does your mother know about this?"

"She doesn't see anything. Papi got mad, though. He went to his house and told him to stay away from me." Marielos pulled away, stepped over the gutter and onto the sidewalk, and kept walking.

"Does he?"

"No. I see him almost every day. Papi's never here to notice, and Mami only cares about Papi being here and the baby. And when he is here they just shut themselves into the bedroom and do it and do it, big belly and all."

Oscar stopped walking and grunted with disgust.

"Uncle?" Marielos turned around.

"*China*, please do not tell me any more of these things, I don't want to hear any of these things you're telling me."

"Uncle, don't be upset! Nelson treats me very well. I want to marry him so I can get away from Mami. The only problem I have is Mami. I don't like being around her anymore."

"You should honor your mother," Oscar heard himself say. It was something his mother used to say to Vivi.

"I know, but I'm sorry," Marielos said.

Oscar stopped and took her by the arm again. "Listen to me, Marielos. You cannot see this Nelson anymore, and not because I'm going to tell your parents, but rather because there is only one thing that he's after, and I'm afraid to think..."

With a jerk Marielos reclaimed her arm, doing her best to look annoyed and dignified. "Okay, uncle." She tried to keep her mouth straight, but a smile forced the set line of her mouth to break. All her teeth were showing. The sun shone off her cheeks.

Oscar's heart leather pulled away from its sole. There were so many people he cared for who would not let themselves be saved. They walked straight away from love, down the dark alley, and he could do so little to bring them back. Were his open arms not enough?

No, Oscar thought; they were not. He needed to use those arms better. To pull with them. To use hands, to hold on.

On his next visit to Cinderella's house, Oscar brought two toucans—ten thousand, what Martín charged for the works—and two condoms from the United States, left behind by his former lover, a gringo named Jim. Oscar hadn't had sex since Jim had returned to the States.

They were in a hotel near the Coca-Cola bus station. Oscar couldn't force himself to look away from the dirty sheets at Cinderella's anymore. He'd seen blood once. There was semen and there were other dubious dark circles that the flowered sheets couldn't camouflage. The last time he'd been there to see Martín, he'd gone afterwards into the bathroom to rinse with mouthwash, and when he'd spit into the sink, the mouthwash went right through the tube and landed all over his shoes. That was infuriating, but the sheets were disturbing. When Oscar had asked Martín how often the sheets were changed, he said, "Once a month, unless someone important shows up."

Oscar and Martín smoked cigarettes on the bed, probably for different reasons. "Listen, Oscar, I'm going back now, so where's the money."

"I can walk you back to Cinderella's."

Martín buckled his jeans and clenched his jaw. "No, you can't."

"I'd like to go visit Cinderella, I like him."

"Listen, Oscar, you're good people, but I don't want to hang out with you all the time. I don't understand *tipos* like you. You're masculine, but you're gay. You seem all mixed up, and I'm not in a mood to get mixed up myself."

"I'm not mixed up at all," Oscar said. "You are more mixed up than I am. You have sex with five men a day and you think you're the most macho straight man in San José."

"Hear me. I do it for the money, Oscar, nothing could be more cut and dried."

Oscar looked at the lips he'd never kissed. He wanted to tell Martín something, but knew he should not.

"Do you like doing it?" Oscar asked.

"No, I hate it, but how else can I make money like this? And I have to live somewhere. Cinderella lets me live there for free, but I have to work."

"Where are your parents?"

"My father's in hell, probably, and my mother kicked me out because she caught me smoking grass and decided it was rock. She doesn't know the difference between a joint and a crack bottle."

Oscar had seen Martín smoke off a crack bottle in the salon, but didn't mention it. Instead he said, "My mother is dead."

"You're better off," Martín said.

"Martín, why don't you come live with me? I have an extra room."

"No," he said, his eyes cold. "Give me the money, stop trying to turn me into a faggot, and don't follow me home."

Martín took the money and left, and Oscar did go to Cinderella's, but Martín did not come back for the rest of the afternoon. Oscar spent his day off in Cinderella's kitchen, chewing spearmint gum to keep the heartsickness from rising into his mouth.

A hamster cage had appeared next to the hotplate. A blond hamster ran maniacally on its wheel. There was the sound of metal squealing and water dripping from the plastic tube in the sink, and, of course, the scratching sounds of the dogs from inside Cinderella's secret room.

Juan Antonio charged Oscar three hundred colones for a can of Imperial. He was the man who'd been standing in the doorway listening to the Cinderella story, and he told Oscar he was twenty-five, an old man, and not a *cachero*, but straightforwardly gay. "I'm the only gay here, except for William, who lives in the back room and lives for nothing but to eat, sleep, and whore. He actually seems to enjoy it. He's weird."

"Very weird," agreed Flaco, a *cachero* eating toast.

Oscar wanted a second beer but he was running low on money.

"And Cinderella," Oscar said, "with his wicked stepmother who turned him into a *playo* by not letting him play soccer."

Juan Antonio took Oscar's sarcasm as incredulity. "Everything those boys told you is true," he said. "Cinderella has had a horrible life, and he's such a good person. He lived in a tunnel and had to steal off clothes lines when his clothes got too small. All the other *playos* hated him because he was such a beautiful boy."

"So," Oscar said, making light, "Where's the handsome prince?"

Juan Antonio placed his palms on the greasy tabletop and lowered his chin, glaring at Oscar. His nostrils splayed like those of an animal angered by its own fear. "I'M the handsome prince, you fuckhead," he said. Oscar realized his mistake too late; he hurried to erase the smile from his face. Juan Antonio stood up and pushed his chair back so hard it fell, and he left the kitchen without righting it.

Flaco smirked behind his Belmont light. "If you don't watch out, you'll wake up and find that you've been turned into a hamster," he said to Oscar. Flaco chuckled so hard it turned into a cough.

The pool hall next door was a foreboding place. It was a dark room, filled with bad smells, which Oscar knew from the few times he'd ventured into pool halls: they all had the same reek of man-sweat and spilled beer. Oscar hated pool halls because gays were hated in pool halls, as were women. He spat a chewed wad of gum into the street, unwrapped a new stick, and loitered near the doorway, hoping Martín would exit before he started to look too pathetic, waiting there.

A girl in a leotard and jeans sat outside on the step, waiting also, occasionally glancing inside. The door of the pool hall was open, and they could see a group of boys playing pool and pretending not to be aware of being watched. The girl in the leotard was thin, but she looked like she'd swallowed a small papaya sideways.

"Is your boyfriend inside?" Oscar asked her. She glanced at him suspiciously. If her skin had not been ashy, her eyes not dull, she might have been a pretty girl.

"Is yours?" she bit.

Oscar did look inside when she said that, hoping for a glance of Martín. Martín was there, angry-looking, a cue in his hand. He handed the cue to a friend and walked out to the step.

"Karla," he said, and took the girl in his arms. Kissing her with the lips that had never kissed Oscar. His hand resting on her belly.

"What were you waiting for? I need to talk to you inside," Karla said, and they walked back to Cinderella's house without a word to Oscar.

Oscar sat where Karla had sat, trying to feel the warmth her body had left on the concrete, but it was cold. He spat his piece of gum towards the street and reached into his pocket for another stick. The gum landed on the sidewalk. Oscar hoped one of the boys from the pool hall would step in it. Then he realized that was a mean thing to wish for, and stood up, considered the grayish gob on the pavement, wondering if he should pick it up, wrap it in the paper it had come in, and throw it in a trash can. But there were no trash cans in this part of town.

He was still standing there, with his thoughts of gum, when Karla flew out of Cinderella's gate and landed on the sidewalk, falling on her side. She hadn't been shoved hard, but she had been shoved.

"That's it!" Cinderella stood in the doorway with his hands full of clothes. Martín struggled to keep him from throwing them on the sidewalk, too, but they slipped out of Cinderella's grip, article by article. "You stupid slut, you even wore lycra! How stupid do you think I am?"

"Cinderella, those aren't my clothes, they're William's." Martín had Cinderella by the wrist.

"I don't believe you." Cinderella kicked a shirt that had fallen. "Get out, live on the street if you want to, give birth in the gutter. You're spoiled fruit, go rot someplace else!" The gate slammed behind him.

Karla, dusting herself off, was nonplused. "You didn't tell me he'd kick us out if I was pregnant."

Martín helped her off the ground. "What do you think, he wants a baby to be born in the middle of Sin Alley and eaten by dogs? Why'd you wear lycra, *tonta*?"

"You're the one who let me walk in there."

Martín gathered up the clothes from the sidewalk and left them in a pile next to the gate. "William's going to be pissed when he wakes up."

"Where are you going to go?" Oscar asked. They both looked up at him, her eyes curious, his nervous and wide. "I ask because I have an extra room, and you can stay in it if you'd like." He offered them a piece of paper with his address written on it. Karla took it, and looked up at Martín, her brow wrinkled, questioning.

Inside, Oscar found Cinderella crying in front of his altar. Pink and red feathers framed a statue of Changó, the god of fire and thunder. The boys on the couch watched television and ignored Cinderella, or they moved into the kitchen to get away from the sound of his sobs, which distracted them from the pornographic film they'd seen already anyway.

Oscar touched him on the shoulder. Cinderella's face was stricken with a child's sorrow. "I give everything to them. I can't stand to see a kid on the street. And they treat me so badly, they insult me all the time. They hate me just because I want to have nice things and be around beauty. They don't love me."

Cinderella smelled like he hadn't showered in awhile, but Oscar took him into his arms.

"There is love, Cinderella," Oscar said. Cinderella's tears sank into his shirt.

Oscar held him. "I will love you," Oscar said. "I already do." Oscar's own eyes filled with tears.

Summer came to San José in December. The three o'clock rains no longer fell; the air stayed dry and warm all day. Oscar lay in his own bed with Martín. Now that he was taking care of Martín, he didn't have to pay him for each session, and Martín accepted it. It was considered normal for a *cachero* to do this, as long as the money came somehow.

"Do you hate Cinderella?" Oscar asked him. He knew Martín was still whoring there, though Martín pretended not to be.

"Why would I hate him? He's like a mother and a father to me.

He took me in when I had nowhere to go, and he fed me when I had nothing in my belly."

"But what you've had to do."

"What I do is a sin," Martín said, "But God forgives sins when you stop doing them. Isn't it in the Bible like a thousand times?"

There was a quote Oscar knew from Isaiah. He knew it well enough to quote it, and so he did. "God says, 'Wash you, make you clean; put away the evil of your doings from before mine eyes; cease to do all evil; Learn to do well; seek judgment, relieve the oppressed, judge the fatherless, plead for the widow.'"

Martín asked Oscar to repeat this, and Oscar did, and Martín's face went blank for a moment. "What does that mean, 'judge the fatherless'?"

"Call us bastards, I guess," Oscar said.

"Well, I may be a bastard forever, but I won't always be a sinner. I'll have an honest life someday." Martín glared at Oscar. But his eyes were the stones and his cheekbones the sharp blade against them, and sparks lit for a moment before dying in the coldness of Martín's face. "Will you be honest, Oscar?"

Oscar didn't breathe. "I am as honest as I know how to be, Martín." That was a lie designed to make Oscar look righteous. He believed if you said something untrue, you could convince yourself that it was true, and that this was the same thing as telling the truth.

Martín let Oscar kiss him, because now he had no choice.

On Tuesday, Martín left the apartment without saying goodbye while Oscar was in the middle of scrambling the last of the eggs.

"Where are you going?" Oscar called after him, but Martín did not hear him, or ignored him, Oscar didn't know which. He spread a small amount of margarine on a piece of Bredy toast and shoveled the eggs into his mouth like a savage, because no one was there to see the bits of egg caught in the stubble on his chin, or hear the digestive process beginning in his noisy, open mouth. Before Martín had moved in with him, Oscar had always been a neat eater, even at home by himself. But now, though Oscar did not know why, he grew wild when he was alone.

The phone rang and Oscar wiped the egg off his face with a paper napkin. It was Marielos, crying. "Mami pushed me into the barbed wire because she heard I was still seeing Nelson. I have cuts all over my arms."

"Is your father home?"

"Of course he is, that's why I can call you and Mami doesn't even care."

"*China*, why don't you pack some things and come stay with me for awhile. Do you have money for the bus?"

"I can take some out of mami's purse. It's yours, anyway." Oscar didn't correct her. But he hadn't given Vivi money in months, because he didn't have extra to give.

He was not thinking of the stranger Marielos had become. What he was thinking about was getting Marielos, the little girl he loved, away from Nelson, and also that he needed some help with the housework, because Martín was a slob. He let Marielos make plans to catch the bus to the city before he called Vivi to tell her he would look after Marielos for a while.

"I don't really understand what's happened between you two," he told his sister, "but I'll tell you what I do understand. She is still seeing Nelson, and Cartago is no longer a safe place for her."

Vivi sighed. "Take her if you want her," she said. "She'll get tired of hanging around you and all your faggot friends soon enough." Oscar ignored the slur, feeling immensely satisfied. He knew Vivi would have been enraged by his smile if she could have seen it, but she couldn't see it, so Oscar gave himself the allowance of a smile.

When Marielos arrived, Oscar poured hydrogen peroxide on her cuts and bandaged them with gauze, even though the wounds were superficial. Marielos went to sleep in the spare bedroom. Martín came home, wobbling and bumping into things, and Oscar grabbed him by the arm before he could open the door to the room where his niece lay, dreaming of *boli*s and pizzeria restaurants.

"Marielos is asleep in there," Oscar whispered.

"Your girlfriend?" Martín smirked.

"Where's your girlfriend?" Oscar asked, knowing that she was at home, with her parents. They'd taken her back in. Martín couldn't have been out with her; she hated when he drank and smoked drugs. Oscar knew exactly where he had been. Karla still came around sometimes, despite Cinderella's house, despite Oscar himself. Oscar suspected Martín went and saw her while he was at work, and also that she hated Oscar. But he was feeding Karla too, and the growing child—she took his money, hate or not.

It wasn't until Oscar was dressing to go out for groceries the next day, while Marielos lay sleeping in one room, and Martín in the other, that Oscar realized there was something he needed to worry about. He pushed open the door to the spare bedroom.

"*China*," he whispered, shaking Marielos gently awake. She squinted in the darkness and rolled over, away from him. She looked adorable, her hair messy and strands of it tangled near her ear. "*China*," he said, "I'm going to the super. Will you come with me?"

Marielos moaned no.

"Okay, *negra*, but stay in this room, okay? I want you to stay in this room until I get back." But Marielos was pretending to be asleep again. Oscar sighed, and shut the door tightly behind him. At the super, he bought more eggs, some cheese, Corn Flakes, and a box of milk. There would be no more lard-greased gallo pinto for his niece; he would feed her better than Vivi had. Maybe she would even slim down some.

When he entered the apartment, Oscar heard voices coming from his bedroom. He threw the bag on the table, ignoring the fragility of the eggs, and flung open the bedroom door.

Marielos was leaning, hip jutting out, against the wall; Martín was still under the covers, and Oscar hoped that he had his *tangas* on. They stopped talking when Oscar appeared in the doorway. Martín looked slightly annoyed with both of them, but it was always hard to tell with Martín. He pulled the covers up to his chin and shifted.

Oscar took Marielos by the arm. "Go put on a sweater, it's cold," he told her, "and then come help me make the breakfast." He shut the door to his own bedroom, looking inside at Martín as the door swung. Martín was lazy, sly, and sleepy. But Oscar thought he saw a smirk.

"Ay, uncle," Marielos said, cheerfully cracking eggs into a bowl, "You're going to be worse than mami, aren't you?" She smiled with half her mouth.

"*China*, you're walking a dangerous path."

"No I'm not."

Oscar snapped. "Listen, girl, I'm trying to take care of you, so you'd better let me. I am the one who cares about you." He had her by the arm, and was holding her too tight. A bit of eggshell rolled onto the floor. She looked at him with hatred, and tried to pull away, but he wasn't letting go until he was ready to let go.

He released her only when he realized how tight his grip really was. Freed, Marielos rubbed her arm.

"Uncle, just let me be. All I want is to be let alone."

"Okay, then, I'll leave you alone to make breakfast," Oscar said quietly, and went back into his bedroom. He lay down on the bed and poked Martín with his elbow.

"You're still whoring and you're still smoking crack," Oscar said.

"No I'm not," Martín said. "And you're the one walking a dangerous path, not your niece."

"Just stay away from her," Oscar said. Martín lazily raised his middle finger.

At work, Oscar broke a glass and cried over it. The path of sin was well-lit, and the mines were easy enough to step over. You got piss on your shoes just from walking down the street. There was no sense in dwelling over it, Oscar realized, and dried his eyes.

They were at home, the two of them, his lover and his niece. Oscar knew that when there were three of them, one would not belong, and he knew which one had to go.

He arrived home to find them eating buttered saltines at the dinner table. Marielos was wearing the tiniest tank top she owned and leaning over the table towards Martín, which inspired a fresh wave of rage in Oscar, and he realized that would make it easier to do what he had to do. Oscar walked past them to the bathroom and poured hydrogen peroxide over the cut the glass had given him. While the sting lasted, he walked back to the front door, opened it, and fixed his eyes on Marielos.

He pointed to the street and said, "Go."

FLEE

We were always hungry, all of us. We fought over food. We tried to trick each other out of fair shares. Elliot said he had never seen anything like it.

"Most groups have so much extra food they have to bury the leftovers," he'd told us, shaking his head.

Eating, we watched each others' mouths, wondering whose mouth was fullest.

Anna Verges cooked for us. The idea was we would cook together, but as long as Anna did it, no one else had to. She made our dinners, and she got up early to start the stoves. The orange cylinder of strike-anywhere matches was essentially all hers.

Had she asked for help, I would not have offered mine. I was not in training to be another woman in another kitchen. When it was time to clean up, I pretended I had to go to the bathroom and disappeared into the woods.

Anna Verges filled our cups with rice first, and then the vegetables, which had turned a uniform hue, slightly fluorescent, in the soup mix Anna'd added.

"That green powder was pea soup?" Deirdre said, disappointed.

"I was sure it was pistachio pudding."

Some complained about pea soup, how could they give us pea soup when it was something that so many people hated? But when Skylar and Ryan asked for the shares of the complainers, they bent down into their cups and ate.

"Are there any seconds?" Skylar asked. I found a small pebble in my rice and picked it out. Three or four spoonfuls remained in the bottom of my cup; I looked around the tarp for other edibles, and saw none.

"Skylar can't have seconds until the rest of us finish," Ryan protested.

"I was just asking if there WERE any, dickhead," Skylar said.

"No," Anna said, "I dished it all out," which reminded us to thank Anna for cooking.

"I wish I had a cigarette," Carlyn said.

Elliot, trying for irony, said, "That's the attitude," but it came off as condescension. Our other leader, Cath, cleared her throat.

"I wish I had a big slice of peanut butter pie right out of the freezer, with globs and globs of hot fudge on it," Deirdre said, as she licked her spoon clean of pea soup, and looked down into her metal cup to see if there was anything left to scrape out of it.

"That would kill me," Ryan said. His blue eyes came alive in the beam of a headlamp. Someone groaned. "Get that light out of my face," Ryan said, and shielded his eyes with his hand, sending a shadow across himself briefly before Skylar screwed his headlamp off.

"I'm going to kill you if you don't stop talking about what

could kill you," Skylar said, sending Ryan into an instant sulk.

Peanuts were dangerous to Ryan. Kitchens were dangerous to me. Drugs of any kind were dangerous to Jim Jacobis, a skinny guy from Alabama who was here because of them. His counselor said Rehab or FLEX; his parents said choose, and Jim chose FLEX because it came without twelve steps or therapy, and he wasn't ready to give up drugs, or even think about it hard.

"Percocets and a twelve-pack would be nice," Jim said, looking at Elliot, and smirked.

"Someday I'll tell you what that does to your blood pressure," Elliot said, looking dark and frustrated, like a kid squirming in a dirty diaper, unable to articulate his discomfort.

"Which might give me a whole new reason to do it," Jim said.

"Jim," Carlyn said, warning him. If he talked like this too much, Cath and Elliot might go through his bags.

Skylar was here because he'd dropped out of college and didn't know what else to do. Carlyn was here because she'd dropped out of college and was trying to figure out what to do next. I was here because I'd dropped out of college and was trying to figure out how to get back. I'd liked school. What had gone wrong?

In the beginning we were eleven, but a couple who'd come together had been kicked off for having sex, and now we were nine.

Anna Zec was lost and sad. Veronica didn't want to go to college at all, but didn't know how to have a job, didn't feel ready; she was seventeen, and where she was from no one worked a real job until they were at least twenty, done with college. Deirdre was using this as her Semester Abroad, and was even getting college credit for it. Cath and Elliot led trip after trip.

"It sure beats being in an office," Elliot had said, at the top of a peak, while the rest of us glared at him, sucking for breath.

The official acronym of Florida Expeditions was FLEX, but in the outside world we called it FLEE.

But there was Anna, Anna Verges, who did yoga stretches on her sleeping mat before she rose to start the pots boiling and stayed serene all day. We didn't trust her. Her unruly armpit hair had alienated the boys the minute they laid eyes on her, in the airport, where Anna Verges had hovered at the periphery of our circle in a pair of shorts that already looked dirty.

Anna Verges. She was the last one eating while the rest of us rubbed our cups out with water and pine needles. She knew how to measure out the bites, make it last. She knew no greed. We turned our backs on her, because she made us look bad. Only the maladjusted were social with her, and Anna returned their stabs at kindness; you could tell she didn't know how to do otherwise.

"Who's going to clean up?" Cath asked, and was greeted with silence.

"I will," Anna Verges said. Anna Zec, who was off-kilter, friendless, offered to help. Anna Zec had chunks of hair missing because she had decided to cut it all off, but the scissors on her Swiss Army knife were tiny, ineffectual, and cutting with them was tedious; they sliced through only a few strands at a time, and she made the first cut without considering this. She cut it off bit by bit, in shifts. Sometimes, Anna Verges helped her, cutting the places in back where Anna Zec couldn't reach.

Veronica gave names to people: Anna Zec was Flipper for the many times she'd flipped. Skylar was The Bullet for his tenacity and speed. Anna Verges was Mom.

"Thanks for dinner, Mom." The boys went to the sleeping tarp. If I ever entered the kitchen tarp to work, I would do it only after every boy had done it first. I would not clean for any man before he cleaned for me.

Here is the one thing I would do: fill the water jugs down at the river. Veronica and I volunteered to fill the water jugs every night because Veronica had smuggled in a pack of Marlboros in a Ziplock bag and the river was way down trail, where they wouldn't be able to smell us. We cleaned our cups, took the four empty jugs, and hiked down the trail, stopping for our fleece jackets. It was getting cold, even in Tennessee; it was early October. We were somewhere in the mountains. Our landscape was a densely-treed pocket of the South with trails cut through it by decades of hikers. The treetops were so tall it was usually hard to locate a peak; we were always lost because of this. There were snake dens and bees' nests and magical-seeming caterpillars with bright bodies and stingers. Branches grazed our arms as we hiked. It rained here more than it didn't. If you had handed me a map five miles wide and asked me to pinpoint our location, I could do it, as long as I had a compass and had been paying attention during the last hike. If you'd handed me a map of Tennessee as asked me to point to the general area of our campsite, I'd be lost.

*

Veronica was a spoiled girl from northern California, freckled, adorable, a baby. She missed her stereo, her television shows, and the smell of her mother's laundry soap. "Should we smoke another one?" Veronica always needed someone to tell her when to stop.

"We only have ten cigarettes left," I said.

"How many days until break?" Veronica asked, counting the cigarettes to be sure and putting them back in the pocket of her fleece jacket.

"Twenty-three," I said. "Isn't it interesting, how they make these sessions the length of a menstrual cycle?"

"Fascinating, Zoe. Be sure to tell that one to Jim and Skylar."

I closed my lips. I was about to bleed, then; I could feel the tug on my nipples, the cringing in my uterus. It was the time I most craved contact with skin, and when the blood came, I would crave the thrust; and I would not hide my blood, especially not from the ones who feared it, who reveled, glibly, in that learned disgust.

"Misogyny," I muttered.

"Huh?" Veronica said, with a tone that meant she didn't really want to know.

For now, I opened my lips only to blow smoke. Honesty only got you so far when you were trying to make friends. Veronica was a friend I made over cigarettes and shared interests: we both wanted spots at the center of the tarp, and took turns saving each other places. She was hilariously funny, especially on the trail when humor was most needed, and told stories in a confident raspy voice.

Veronica and I filled the water jugs, giddy from the nicotine, in the shallow part of the river, where it ran fast. We counted twenty drops of iodine into each, and left them in the kitchen tarp for Anna Verges to boil for breakfast. The sediment began to sink.

I crawled into my bag in the middle of the tarp, the only position I would tolerate, surrounded by bodies on both sides, and took off everything except my underwear and turtleneck, stuffing it all into the sleep sack that was also my pillow. Skylar had already lifted his arm for me to crawl into his armpit, and as I snuggled in he reached for my breast over the slippery sleeping bag, and we kissed once, a long kiss, his growing beard scratching like hairbrush bristles pressed into my skin, making no noise at all, so silent that we could hear Anna Verges, alone in the kitchen tent, scraping out the pots, one of which had a burned bottom; she'd never get that pot clean. I fell asleep to cicadas and strange tree creaks and the scrape, the scrape of Anna Verges's endurance.

Veronica was like the rest of us: coddled, tired, shocked by what was being asked of our bodies. Anna Verges was not.

Anna Verges had big, black eyes so dark the target of her pupil was lost. She was small and lithe, tiny, but strong; the hair that grew under her arms and like fur on her legs gave her a sense of virility. She was flexible and had what Elliot called "core strength," meaning she could take a big, uneven step up a chunk of rock with ease and grace when the rest of the girls had to scramble up using our hands. She smelled like she'd crawled out of an ocean, briny and ripe.

When I tried to talk to her, I couldn't get my tongue out of the way. It was swollen with the salt that I knew was on Anna's skin.

Anna Verges came from a family of hippies who lived in Vermont. She slept naked, but she wanted to run naked, swim naked, just be unwrapped; only under the cover of her sleeping bag was this allowed.

"There are a few reasons why nakedness is prohibited," Cath said. "The first one is in case hunters accidentally stumble on us." We had to wash in our jog bras and underwear, when we got a chance to wash. It frustrated Anna, and she washed naked when she thought no one was looking. I did look. She was stunning, animal, as she squatted to dip her long hair in the water, her knees apart.

Anna hadn't eaten meat in seven years. She didn't care that we weren't allowed to wash our hair. She didn't wear deodorant.

"All it does is attract bugs," Anna said. "You're going to smell anyway."

Veronica covered herself with deodorant just to spite Anna, putting it behind her knees, behind her neck, and woke up covered in welts.

Anna knew because she'd lived outside before. She'd spent months sleeping in a tent, following the Grateful Dead with her sister, Jessica, and her adopted sister, Naomi, which is what she'd been doing before she'd come to FLEE.

No one knew exactly what I'd been doing before Tennessee. I thought it would be best to keep it brief. I said, "I lived in New York," which impressed them; they were from Iowa, New Hampshire, Alabama, the suburbs of New Jersey. I'd said, I'd lived in a dorm my freshman year, and then I'd moved into an apartment in the East

Village with some friends, which made me sound independent. So far, a good story. I'd told them how I dropped out of school. They nodded their heads.

I even told them about how, in the end of my time in New York, I was smoking pot every day, all day, watching television all day, chain smoking cigarettes, which, after smoking pot, actually felt like they were cleansing my insides; I'd told them how I'd lost interest in things, in school, in my friends—I didn't try to tell them why. Just that I'd wound up back in the house of my childhood. In Darien, Connecticut.

Florida Expeditions cost money. Carlyn had a scholarship, and Jim had paid for half of it himself, out of guilt for what he'd put his parents through. The rest of us were from big houses, white neighborhoods, high tax brackets. We had credit cards in the FLEX house, stored with the rest of the stuff we'd left behind before the course began. This privileged crowd, they chafed at the idea of need. Florida Expeditions was self-punishment, in a way, but it was voluntary. They liked their friends familiar: white, wealthy, straight and kind. I played the role and the costume scratched and strangled.

For starters, I was not always kind.

Anna Verges played no role.

"Sometimes, I feel like I should be at home," Anna said on the trail. "I miss my sister Jessica. I feel like she needs me right now. Naomi's about to take off, hitchhike to California, and I'm afraid Jessica's going to drop out of high school and go with her."

Veronica looked at me and rolled her eyes. "Imagine that was your life," she muttered, out of Anna's earshot. "When I go home, all I'm going to be concerned about is how fast my mom can do my laundry."

She snorted, thinking my home was like her home.

My mother grew up in Brooklyn in a cramped duplex and dreamed of somewhere green and tree-lined. She had two brothers and a sister. She dreamed of space. My father was a Connecticut man. He worked in computers, which, in his generation, was a profession for nerds. Some might say my father was a nerd, but any negative implications of the term were eclipsed by the amount of money his nerdy qualities eventually generated. Throughout his twenties he commuted to New York City every morning, put in his time, and eventually started his own small company. He had an idea of what was coming. He had access to the Internet while his Darien friends were still petrified of word processing, still plucking out their memos on electric typewriters.

He was ten years older than my mother, a big square man with conventional desires: a nice home, a pretty wife, children. My mother was twenty when she married him. She had me and then my brother thirteen months later and, according to her own story, said of motherhood, "This is NOT what I thought it was going to be." Other mothers laugh at this consistently; it's one of my mother's jokes. She resented what was being asked of her, and my father didn't understand. Hadn't she had a mother who'd dropped everything to take care of her?

"Yes," my mother said. "And wasn't she pathetic?" Her mother had had four kids, no money, lost her looks by thirty; every day had been filled with thankless labor. She had made nothing of her life and acquired nothing. She was still in that same shadowy duplex wearing clothes that had no shape, watching crime-show dramas during the dark hours.

Though my mother had no career, she arranged for nannies from European countries so she could live the life she'd wanted, whether my father understood or not. He'd had a mother who relished motherhood. It seemed unnatural to him not to.

It's not like she wasn't a good mother; she just wanted help. Here are some stories of my youth: I went to the zoo and a goat ate the lace hem of my purple dress, and my mother smacked him off and held me while I shook and cried, and then mended the hem. Another animal fiasco: my brother Dustin, in the back yard, age two, sitting in the sand pile with a shovel and a pail, oblivious to the German Shepherd that was charging him, running at Dustin with fangs bared, and my mother flew towards him, screaming, not fast enough to save him, when the dog at the last minute jumped over him and kept running. She picked him up and wouldn't let go for days. There was dress-up. There were lullabies in laps.

There are also stories of a mother sobbing, which is the most terrible sound in the world; the nanny who was addicted to television and frozen Chicken Kiev, which is mostly all she cooked for us; stories of me, a girl with my Barbie dolls, sitting in the tennis pro shop with the macho tennis pro trying to tickle me while my mother was out on the courts. And: the endless yo-yo of being told to eat, not eat, eat, not eat. Or, do either, only be careful how you grow.

Where was my father in these stories?

My father's work hours had grown mysteriously long by the time I was in middle school.

My mother discovered my father's affair while I was in my sixth month at boarding school, which was lucky for me, because after she threatened to leave him and he begged her to stay, she decided that her way to salvation was dedication to a real family, and that meant I got to go home.

I was twelve. I hated boarding school. My first week, a girl named Orly, who'd been there since fourth grade, ordered me to snort a line of cocaine she said she'd gotten from her older brother. I said no and Orly told me I was a pussy and she turned on another new girl, Clara, an anemic-looking blonde whose terrified face I will never forget, who took the rolled ten-dollar bill and snorted what turned out to be Ajax.

The girls there had been orphaned by leisure and frivolity, and they knew it, and they were toxic. I still hoped for love.

Love for me was a door that closed, but never all the way. I could always see a crack of light. My mother cut down on tennis, took cooking lessons, and wore an actual apron. She cooked elaborate meals for us that she never ate herself, instead consuming small platefuls of vegetables that, for my father and me, were side-dishes to roasted lamb and poached fish with rich sauces. My mother helped me with my homework and bought me dresses for Bat Mitzvahs. I was reinstalled at my former school, where my friends had missed me. We wrestled each other to be King of the Mountain, we played lacrosse, we swam on the swim team. I won the 50-meter fly in every race and never got fat, as a girl. But about my broad shoulders, which were good for little more than a flawless butterfly, nothing could be done. And they were inauspicious.

When she came to get me in my East Village apartment, my 19-year-old body swollen beyond the limits of growing girldom, the first thing my mother said was, "Oh Zoe, you're bloated. I'll make you some hot lemonade." What she meant was, there was no way I could really be that fat—I must be retaining water. She went out to the deli for lemons and Sweet-n-Low, along with a roll of Tums, since the lemonade always sent acid to my mouth.

At home, she fed me low-fat meals of baked chicken, wheat pasta with oil-free marinara, steamed squash, and I raided the cabinets for tins of salted nuts that were sent as holiday gifts and never opened.

My mother's learned officiousness had compounded my father's domestic inertia. In the house, he did nothing. I never once, before the affair or after, saw him so much as clear his plate from the table. He never learned to operate the coffee maker, this man who worked with machines, though he drank two cups of coffee every morning. He sat at the breakfast table with a bowl of cereal, blindly eating spoonfuls while reading off the screen of his portable computer, until my mother emerged in her bathrobe, make-up-less, groggy. She didn't eat breakfast, herself; she rose simply to grind coffee beans, pour water, and flick the switch to ON. A few times, when my mother dallied, my father asked me if I wanted any coffee. As in, do you want to make it for me.

"I'll show you how," I offered, and he said, "Oh, that's okay babe," and turned back to his computer.

I knew what it was like to want something, to have it so close, and to have to wait for it. Watching someone hog the joint. Knowing the bowl was almost empty, that someone had a bag in the pocket of their jean jacket, and praying they would pack the bowl again before you had to ask. This—my father waiting for someone else to operate the machinery that would provide him with his drug—was true laziness.

I would never be that lazy.

I would never make coffee for any man who hadn't made me coffee first.

I made myself a cup of black tea, and drank it across the table from my father, who pretended not to hear my dainty slurps.

It was not the coffee that lured Skylar to me, but the coffee helped. I didn't intend it. It was because of the coffee.

I had a double-baggie filled with grounds of Taster's Choice, which I'd smuggled in for the specific purpose of bartering. I didn't drink coffee. I had to keep it in two baggies to keep the smell from leaking out. Caffeine was against the rules.

"It's a drug like any other drug," Cath had said. "It's a crutch."

Anyone found in possession of drugs would be kicked off. Anyone so much as chewing tobacco products, kicked off. Anyone engaged in intimacy—gone.

"Another crutch," Cath said, to our astounded faces. It was the first day of a six week course. We had already started looking each other over.

Anna Verges assented vocally, while the rest of us squirmed on the rock-riddled ground.

She was not in our circle on the fourth day when Ryan said, "Okay, whoever has anything illicit to share, spill it."

Veronica had the cigarettes and she said nothing.

"I have my body," Deirdre said.

Veronica also had a couple of Vicodins she didn't mention, left over from a wisdom tooth extraction.

Jim had pot that he planned to share later, but for now he kept it to himself, smoking it at night, far away from the rest of us, just before crawling into his sleeping bag.

"I have Taster's Choice," I said, and after four days of peppermint tea and splitting packets of hot chocolate that was always too watery, I got offers. A cup's worth for a day's snack. A cup's worth for being allowed to wear Jim's clean socks for one day, as long as I washed my feet in the river first with Doctor Bronner's.

"I'll take the whole bag," Skylar said. "I'll trade you for unlimited full-body massages, any time you want them." Jim stared. Veronica stared. I shook his hand and sealed the deal.

Deirdre had one candy bar she was willing to trade something for, which meant she had more than one hidden in her pack.

"What kind of candy bar?" Ryan asked.

"Snickers," Deirdre said. "It would kill you."

Suddenly I regretted having traded in all of the only thing I had to offer. "Wait," I said. "How many cups' worth do you want for half the Snickers?"

"I'm not interested in coffee," Deirdre said, and Skylar said, "Hey."

"You don't know how much is in the bag anyway," I said. I racked my brain and came up with nothing else I could trade. Frustrated, I said, "Fine." Later, in private, I planned to beg one of the candy bars that Deirdre had but wasn't mentioning. For now, I said, "Okay, Skylar, let's initiate our trade," and we went back to the sleeping tarp, and he straddled me as I lay on my stomach, my face mashed into my sleep sack, his weight on my hips.

Skylar, The Bullet, was not my type. As far as boys went, I preferred them skinny, agile, something pretty in the lips or eyes. In other words, I liked my boys to be more like girls. Skylar was squat, muscular, incredibly quick; he was shorter than I was, which was okay, but there was something simian about his face, and the beard he was growing only made it more pronounced.

But his hands on my body were generous. He was a man who enjoyed using his strength. When we crossed rivers, he was the one who balanced on rocks over the water, offering his arm to grip for balance. He helped us on with our heavy packs, lifting them for us so we could struggle into the straps. Anna Zec always waited near her pack for him. She hiked behind him so he would hold her hand over the log bridges. When he didn't, she fell, though there never seemed to be a reason for her spill—no stick out to trip her, no slippery rock. Without Skylar, Anna Zec just fell.

Skylar was impatient with our pace. He wanted to feel the burn in his muscles, to go faster. With food, he was the greediest. He knew he needed it, needed it more than I did, than Veronica, than Anna Verges; he needed it so he could burn.

His hands found the knots in my muscles and pushed. He kneaded me. I moaned. I told myself what I felt was not lust, but comfort, relief.

I thought, this will be as far as it goes, and didn't believe myself.

I told myself, I am a lesbian who is attracted to men.

This was a true statement, and the source of much confusion. This was one of the reasons things in New York had started to fall apart. With Skylar's knees pressing against my ribcage, I thought of Jocelyn, the girlfriend I had left, and knew it was partly she I'd been fleeing. I'd fled back to this—a boy's weight on top of me—it feeling good. I called it atavism and tried not to let it bother me.

In the mornings, Skylar pretended to want hot water for peppermint tea, and took his mug far away from the rest of us so we couldn't smell his coffee. Watching him at the edge of camp, satisfied, smiling into his cup, I wondered if I hadn't wanted some of that coffee after all.

Breakfast was Grape Nuts in hot water. Grits with butter, salt and pepper. Cream of wheat with raisins and milk powder. Brown sugar on everything—even, sometimes, the grits. It had nothing to do with taste. We would eat anything that converted to energy, of which we always needed more.

My lungs were still healing. I was slow on the trail, and always walked last, with Elliot behind me. On the first hike, we took a break for water, and just as I'd begun to catch my breath, everyone else was screwing on the tops of their water bottles and zipping them back into side pockets, ready to go.

I couldn't say "Wait." I couldn't be the one.

Instead, I panicked. My throat filled with the smell of dirt, of dying leaves, of ammonia. I forced a step, thinking, I can't breathe. Then, I couldn't stop my breath; it came in huge heaves, and I swooned.

"She's hyperventilating," Veronica said, alarmed. "We need a paper bag!"

I fell, pulled backwards by the weight of my pack, and I landed on it, relieved to be supine. Elliot arrived at my side and told me when to inhale and then when to let it out. The panic subsided. I watched Elliot's freckled hands join in a casual prayer position as he rested his elbows on his knees in a comfortable squat. I wanted him to hold me, to stay in control of me, and I breathed as he told me to. I felt better; the others took off their packs and sat down on top of them, grateful for the rest. But now they all knew the truth: I was weak.

I heard Ryan say to Veronica, "A paper bag? Where do you think we are, the cafeteria?" and laugh. I thought, Asshole. I fantasized about hacking off his long blond hair with scissors.

Cath eventually told me I needed to walk in the front. I wouldn't. "I'm too slow," I said, whining and hating myself.

"That's why you need to be up there, setting the pace," Cath said. She was a muscular woman with deep scars on one cheek from a motorcycle accident. I knew she was a dyke. She didn't know I was. She thought I was a little girl, because I was acting like one, and I was making her impatient.

"We're in this together," Cath said. "We're a team. Your pace is our pace. Go up front."

I said, "I'll think about it," and slouched on my pack, and pouted.

Cath sighed.

I thought about it. Anna Verges always walked third.

I said, "Okay. I'll go fourth."

Cath looked over at a tree and said, "Well, I guess that's progress."

Knees twisted; feet burned and blistered. I learned not to be bothered by the sound of my own breath, which was heavy and obscene. I struggled to not be seen struggling.

Anna Verges turned around and said, "You're doing well." I felt patronized and stuck my chin up in the air.

I watched her legs: they were muscular, strong. Anna was so small, you could barely see her beyond her pack; she was two strong legs, in constant motion. She removed branches from her path and held them so they wouldn't swing back on me.

"Thanks," I said. "I can't speak," I said, huffing, "So you tell me a story."

Anna told me about touring with her sister and Naomi. "We lived on yogurt and granola," she said. "I fell in love," she said.

"Where is he now?" I asked. Edward was in Nepal. He had wanderlust and, of course, a beard. I didn't want to hear any more about Edward. "Tell me about your sister and Naomi," I said.

"Naomi moved in with us when she was sixteen," she said. "Her parents were awful. They mentally abused her." I waited for her to explain; Anna didn't. This was insufficient information, as far as I was concerned, but I stored it away to discuss later. Where I grew up, parents didn't just let other people raise their children, but there was plenty of "mental abuse." "I have pictures of them, Jessica and Naomi, if you want to see."

When we camped, as I was securing a place in the center of the sleeping tarp, Anna came over with photographs in a Ziplock bag. She never slept under the tarp unless it was raining; she slept naked under the stars. Twisting on her Petzl, she illuminated a photograph of two ratty girls, bent over a bowl of granola in yogurt, and I recognized an odd urge: I wanted to know these dust-blushed girls. One looked like Anna Verges, though not as dark, her hair in dreads. They smiled together, looking into the bowl. Behind them was a world of tents and weeds and Grateful Dead music.

I wanted to be with them, in a field of foot-mashed grass, eating granola with a communal spoon.

In Connecticut, where I'd grown up, the hippies were all fakes, all Laura Ashley skirts and trust-funded drug binges, and so this was a new feeling. If I'd longed for the time when it had been real, which I had to my mother more than once, she'd said, "Oh, everyone idealizes the Sixties, but it wasn't all peace and love. With all that free sex stuff, I had to tell guys I was a lesbian just to get them to keep their hands off me."

I'd wondered—Did it work?

Under the tarp, my insufficient imitation Petzl lit on these girls and I wondered, was it nice there, with these girls, with their tents and dirty feet?

"I miss Jessica, I miss her a lot," Anna said. There was the love. I had never had a sister.

Then Anna showed me a picture of Edward, his visage obscured by a mass of facial hair, a dumb smile on his face, and I hated hippies again.

"By the way," Anna said, addressing our tarp at large. "I think it's time that we divided into cooking crews. I'm tired of doing all the work by myself."

Twelve eyes blinked in the dark. I twisted off my headlamp.

"You're right, Anna," Deirdre said, and broke twigs into straws that we could draw.

I drew dinner crew. I cut a large block of cheese into small squares, eating them when I thought no one else was looking.

"Stop eating the cheese, Zoe," Ryan said, stirring a pot of mangled spaghetti.

"Here," I said, and handed him two squares. He looked around and popped them into his mouth. I gave two squares to Carlyn before she could protest.

Cath came over to observe our progress. We had been adamant that we did not belong in the kitchen. "It seems to be going all right," she said, smiling in that leaderly way that always intended well, but translated badly.

"I can't believe you are supporting me being another woman in another kitchen," I said. "You, Cath, of all people." Cath looked perplexed. It drove me out of my mind that Cath and I could not communicate, even in code. "I'm not cooking again until all the other boys cook first," I added.

"Are you sure there are no peanuts in this sauce?" Ryan said.

Carlyn was stirring the sauce over a low flame. "For fuck's sake, Ryan," she said, and slumped over the saucepan, a few strands of hair landing in the sauce. From under her hair she mumbled, "Shut up. Just shut up about the peanuts."

Ryan threw the metal spoon on the floor of the tarp. It hit an open Swiss Army knife and clanged dully. I slowly dragged the pot top, upon which I'd been cutting the block of cheese, and inched away with it. Cath crossed her arms and stared. We were in the middle of the woods, of nowhere. What was she going to do?

"Listen, bitch," Ryan said, "I just don't feel like dying, okay? Because that's what will happen if I eat ONE PEANUT, do you understand?"

Carlyn's eyes filled with tears. She stood up, ducking so her head would not hit the tarp.

"Zoe, don't let the sauce burn," she said, and left.

"You're an asshole, Ryan," I said, and he left me to finish dinner by myself. "Fuck you, Zoe, you fucking Feminazi," he said on the way out, and I mutely stirred the sauce, wanting it to boil.

Cath showed me how to drain pasta and turn off the stoves without causing them to explode. Everything turned out entirely edible. I was amazed.

Ryan apologized to Carlyn and me after dinner. "No one understands what it's like to constantly fear death," he said.

"We understand, Ryan," Deirdre said, and rubbed his arm. Carlyn and I crossed our arms and looked at each other.

I snuggled into Skylar's armpit in the tarp, and pulled my sleeping bag up to my head, trying to smother my ears against the sound of Veronica snoring. Skylar reached for my body over the sleeping bag. Everyone else was asleep; we'd learned how to wait. But that night I didn't want him to touch me. I just wanted his warmth.

I pulled his hand to my clavicle, over the polypropylene turtleneck I wore to sleep, and held it there. He accepted my signal and I felt I could release my hold. But then I changed my mind and brought his hand down to the stretch of belly where my turtleneck ended.

Then I heard Anna Zec's breathing, the forced volume of it, and realized she was only pretending to sleep. I clenched Skylar's hand on my belly, and we lay very still.

The time I spent with Anna Verges was behind her, on the trail. She reached out her hand to help me across river stones. Her hand was like a child's.

Walking, we played games to pass the time. One of them was "Name things Ryan can't eat or else he'll die."

Peanuts. Peanut butter. Peanut brittle. Peanut butter pie. African Peanut Soup (that was Anna Verges's). Pad Thai. Any ice cream served in an ice cream parlor, except soft serve, which couldn't be contaminated by the scoop. Kentucky Fried Chicken. Peanut oil. Peanut M&M's. Plain M&M's. Butterfingers.

"One of the worst things that ever happened to me was the McFlurry," Ryan said. "McDonald's used to be one of the only places where it was safe for me to eat anything, and not worry about what kind of oils they have in the kitchen, or how clean the rag is that they're using to clean the tables."

We listened to any story told while we walked. Distraction was necessary; in silence, we felt the pain of our bodies, simultaneous pinprick signals of distress from every point of our bodily star—the greatest, most constant pain in our feet. The night before, when we freed them from their boots and socks, we compared and discovered that not one of us had a pinkie toe anymore. We each had a mashed nub, wrinkled and white, totally flat on the outside, not even there.

Even Anna Verges could not believe our feet.

"So then they got the McFlurry," Ryan said, "And of course, they use Butterfingers in them, and M&M's. Next time you go into McDonald's, watch how they do it. They have this McFlurry machine right over the cups, the drink cups, Butterfinger chips flying everywhere. They get in the Cokes. I can't even sit at a table, in case someone spilled a McFlurry on it before I sat down."

At lunch break Ryan showed us his Epi-Pen, which he would use in case of accidental ingestion.

"Don't touch it," he said, before anyone had lifted a hand. "It'll make the needle shoot out."

Anna Zec reached out to touch it and Ryan pulled it away.

"What happens if you get stuck with it when you don't need it?" asked Anna Zec. She had a horrible design of black and blue and pink under her left eye, from a slip on a log bridge. She had fallen face-down and her pack had come down on the back of her head and smashed her face into the wood. Her eye barely opened. It was worse the morning after, and Skylar and Ryan thought it was funny to make wife-beating jokes. "Yo, get me some chicken pot pie, bitch!" Skylar had said, and then they were volleying. "You guys are fucking assholes," I said, and for once Cath backed me up. "Violence against women is really not funny," she said. Skylar and Ryan looked at us like we'd just let our dog shit on their rug.

"You get all jittery, like a rush of adrenaline," Ryan said, looking at Anna Zec cautiously, capping the Epi-Pen and putting it away. "It's not fun, Anna." Anna Zec was accident-prone and once made a reference to a time she'd swallowed a lot of pills, though we gathered from the vagueness of that noun that she'd swallowed Advil or aspirin. Still, she was hard to predict.

"This is boring," Jim said. "We need a new riddle."

Anna Zec had one. "A man and his son get in a car accident. The father dies and the son is rushed to the hospital. When he gets to the emergency room, the doctor says, 'I can't operate. That's my son.'"

"It's his stepfather," I tried.

Anna Zec's mouth opened wide. "I can't believe you," she said. "You, Zoe, of all people."

"What?" I said, and then it clicked.

I sputtered, "But, see, just the fact that it's a riddle—"

"Of all people," Anna Zec said. Her eyes glowed, victorious. She'd never wanted to be the only one who slipped.

When climbing rock, Anna Zec was not the person you wanted holding your ropes.

You wanted Anna Verges. You could weigh more than she did—all of us weighed more than Anna—and she would still catch you. She felt every tug of the rope, knew your progress, held tight with her gloved hand.

Anna Verges laced her climbing shoes, ate an apple, tied in, and climbed up the Chimney, using her legs where the rest of us would have struggled with our arms. Her legs stretched high. She climbed like a spider, as if it were natural for her to progress vertically, passing Carlyn, who was paralyzed under a ledge on a parallel climb, shaking so hard we noticed it from the ground.

I climbed like Carlyn climbed—terrified, angry, and trembling. Climbing, your demons found you; they tried to pry your fingers from the rock, which only made you cling more fiercely to the rough stone. Hands bled, nails broke, muscles seized. Voices spoke. *You can't do it.*

While I climbed, I felt tears running down my cheeks, though I had not remembered starting to cry.

Each climb got higher until Cath and Elliot took us to the top of an actual cliff. We looked down one hundred and fifty feet, out over the Tennessee pines. Elliot sat at the edge of the cliff, tied in, and one by one, we sat next to him, and then we jumped.

"Touch my hand with your forehead," he said, and trying to reach it from where I sat, I fell off the edge. I caught myself with the rope, and repelled down, wondering where the fear had gone.

Veronica was waiting at the bottom, hidden in a bush and smoking a cigarette.

"How many are left?" I asked.

"This is the last one," she said, and I saw that she was lying. She must have been hiding a second pack all along.

Veronica and I had abandoned our smoking chats after I'd handed her a bag of snacks to tie, said "Tie this," without a please, and she'd said "What, did my skin change color?" She was angry with me for being appalled because it made her feel like a racist. We continued to make each other laugh, but the friendship had become strained.

We sat on a slab of rock in the shade, and it sucked the heat out of us wherever our flesh made contact. I hugged my scabbed knees to my chest.

"Carlyn will take forever, we know that," Veronica said. We watched Anna Zec fall before Elliot even reached up his hand. Their forms were silhouettes blocking the sun. "The Flipper doesn't care if she dies, so she went in 2.5 seconds, probably before she checked to make sure her carabiner was screwed in."

Ryan refused to lean out, and we watched Elliot talk him into it somehow. Then came Anna Verges.

I was getting cold from waiting.

"Brave little Anna Verges," Veronica said. "Thirty seconds, tops."

But Anna Verges would not jump.

Ryan joined us, sweating, on the slab, seeming pleased with himself. He recognized our wonderment. He turned his head to see what we saw.

"Would you look at that," he said, awed as well, looking up at Anna, who was immobile.

Anna Verges had a weakness. Everyone was delighted that Anna had done the worst at something, except for Anna, who was sullen in the van on the way back to base camp, mute and miserable, a smear of grey dirt on her cinnamon cheek.

I thought, If there is a crack, there is something that fingers can slip into, something that can be pried open.

Climbing, my demons had found me, and they found a comfortable spot behind the cage of my ribs, and they grabbed onto the bones and rattled.

I thought, I could love her, Anna Verges. Her black hair was tangled and her hand was buried inside it, frozen in the posture of remorse, as she weakly blinked over her blank stare. Darkness spread inside her; I could see it, and the way it could not leak out. All because she'd held us up. Been afraid.

I thought, Anna, I could help you.

In the morning, I woke up to the dim blue light against my lids and the sound of Deirdre stuffing her sleeping bag into its sack. Skylar rustled beside me. Then he was on top of me, with all of his weight, and I felt his huge erection against my thigh.

"What are you doing?" I pushed him off. Deirdre paused with

her foot inside her sleep sack and looked at us, her eyebrows raised.

"There are people everywhere," I hissed. I was still mad at him about the chicken pot pie, and he had never made a move in broad daylight before. We could get sent home, and I didn't want to go home.

Skylar rose and shook off dramatically. "I can't take this," he said, and reached for the toothbrush propped inside his boot.

Anna punished herself by taking extra weight. In her pack she fit two pots, a stove, and two blocks of cheese, which no one wanted to carry because of the smell it left behind. She tied the garbage to the outside of her pack. Veronica claimed the shovel, which we used for digging holes to shit in, and felt that was enough of a burden; Anna Verges had taken the stove Veronica usually carried.

"Let's go, let's go!" Skylar implored, but we were waiting for Deirdre to get back with the shovel. "Why does it take everyone twenty minutes to take a shit?"

"I'd take a shit right in front of you, if you all weren't so squeamish," Anna Verges said. "Deirdre hiked all the way up trail so no one would see her, but what difference does it make?"

"That's absolutely lovely, Anna," Veronica said. "I'd love to see shit coming out of your ass. That would be the perfect way to start my day."

Skylar and Ryan snickered like schoolboys, and Anna Verges didn't care.

On the trail, the boys blazed. They were tired of reaching camp after dark and having to make camp by the light of headlamps, which made mosquitoes and no-see-ums fly into our eyes. Chivalry had gone out the window when they realized there was no way to get ass.

Carlyn struggled. She was a quiet girl from Iowa, a blonde who rarely spoke, and she had two quirks: on tuna day, no one was allowed to talk to her for an hour after lunch—she had an irrational fear of tunafish; and also, no one was allowed to pass her on the trail.

"It fucks with my sense of competence," she explained in Circle.

"In general, it's good hiking etiquette, not to pass," Cath had said, and we had agreed. We wouldn't pass her. We wouldn't pass any person struggling. We would respectfully meet that person's stride.

But Carlyn slowed drastically on uphill climbs, and on this day, Ryan decided to overtake her.

We heard: "Ryan, don't pass me," between wheezing breaths. But Ryan was already at her side.

Carlyn was tearing, we could hear it in her voice. "Don't you fucking pass me, Ryan," upset and threatening, but her breath picked up. I felt the swimming in her head.

Ryan turned to her, his anger unleashed. We could all hear him scream, "Oh, okay, Carlyn, we'll just cater to you, Carlyn, we'll just do whatever's best for YOU." His pale face had gone pink. His eyes were wild. Carlyn swooned and fell into the rhododendrons, and hung there, suspended by her pack, sobbing and gasping for breath.

Deirdre peeled an orange. "You just need some sugar," she

said, and glared up at Ryan, who was acting concerned, but refused to apologize.

Skylar and Ryan complained to Elliot. "The girls are too slow. We're always lost and we're always late and they're holding us up."

We were eating lunch at the side of the river. I tore off a chunk of my precious bagel and threw it at Skylar, hitting him in the face. Veronica laughed, but it wasn't funny.

That night, I didn't sleep in the tarp. I dragged my mat out where Anna Verges slept next to Ryan and collapsed there, next to Anna.

"I want to go home," I said.

"Hey now, Zoe, I thought you only whined on the trail and in the kitchen," Ryan said.

"Anna," I said, "make him go away."

"I keep trying," Anna said, "but he keeps coming back." I could feel her smile in the dark. She put her hands in my hair, which had grown and was greasy, filthy, filled with river water scum and dirt. Anna Verges didn't mind; she rubbed my scalp until I was suppressing sounds that batted their wings against my throat, wanting out.

"Sometimes, I want to go home too," Anna said. "I got a letter from home when we got resupplied. Naomi's gone. I'm worried that Jessica will be gone before I get back."

"You miss her," I whispered, my eyes closed, every nerve on my scalp alive.

"Yes," Anna said. Then, "Who do you miss?"

"I miss my girlfriend," I said. "But I also don't miss her. Oh, I'll explain later," I said, and fell promptly asleep.

I dreamed of Jocelyn, the one I'd left, but it was not Jocelyn's face I saw when I woke up, it was not Skylar's; it was Anna Verges's. Her long dark hair stretched out behind her. Her eyes were huge and brown, open, on me.

"Hello," I said.

"You were grinding your teeth," Anna said. "I had to rub your chin to get you to stop."

I reached up to feel my chin.

"I had a dream about you," she said. A wall of sand eroded.

The light was blue, crepuscular. Birds called in stray chirps. It was twenty minutes before Skylar's wristwatch alarm would beep, our wakeup call.

"Anna," I whispered, "will you teach me how to light the stoves?"

We prepared Cream of Wheat and set the pots boiling for peppermint tea. I learned to light strike-anywhere matches against the sole of my unlaced boot.

"I miss my girlfriend who is not my girlfriend anymore," I told Anna Verges. "Her name is Jocelyn."

Anna blinked, a normal blink, and placed a lid on a pot.

She said, "Hm." I thought I saw her sniff the air.

"Tell me about her," Anna said, but Deirdre had appeared at the edge of the kitchen tarp, looking at me, perplexed as she had been when Skylar rolled on top of me.

"Zoe?" she said, incredulous, and I said, "Cream of Wheat?" and lifted a lid.

That night, I put my fingers in Anna's hair as she'd put hers in mine. It was stiff and matted. My fingers found fragments of leaves. I touched her face, but did not linger there. Ryan shifted in his sleeping bag as we whispered to each other in the dark.

Anna slept with her face towards me. I watched her face sag into helpless, loose abandon. Her throat thickened with breath.

Mrs. Taylor was an old woman too weak to do her own yard work, and though this seemed like a bizarre form of community service, FLEE sent Tennessee-based groups there at the end of a phase, as a reward.

"She makes a feast," Cath said. "She cooks all day for FLEX groups." Our mouths watered as we hacked weeds and pulled vines out of Mrs. Taylor's trees.

"This is Tennessee," Deirdre reminded us. "She's probably making fried chicken."

We used her bathroom, which had soft toilet paper and a sink decorated with flower-shaped cakes of pink soap. A line formed outside the door. We could not get enough clean, sediment-free tap water. We left dirty puddles under the soap roses and dried our hands on a soft, clean towel.

The Annas dug potatoes out of the ground and Carlyn and Elliot killed a wasps' nest with gasoline. We watched the wasps stagger around the nest, drunk. We looked at the sky, still unable to tell time from the sun, but getting better at approximations, wondering how many weeds we were expected to pull before lunch.

We cut the grass with blades, swinging them like golf clubs.

Our energy was boundless. We had one more week of the program, but first we had a night of sleeping in an actual shelter with a real roof and a porch and plumbing. There were even rumors of a bonfire and marshmallows. It was like coming to shore after five weeks at sea. We were impressed with ourselves, and the extent to which our body hair had grown.

The feast was spread across Mrs. Taylor's kitchen and seemed endless. Vegetable casseroles with breadcrumb crusts. Jell-o Salad. A glazed ham, pocked with cloves. A mountain of fried chicken.

"FLEX groups love my food!" Mrs. Taylor said proudly, showing us photo albums filled with picture of groups like ours, with her in the middle. She made each of us take at least a small helping of salad.

I followed Anna and her plate out to the porch, like a dog hoping for scraps. When I sat down next to her, she smiled and offered me a forkful of ripe tomato. Her plate was full of vegetables.

"I'd like to be a vegetarian," I said, "But I don't like any vegetarian food."

"You don't like anything?" she said.

I thought hard of healthy things. "Yes," I said, brightening. "I really like Breyer's mint chocolate chip ice cream." Anna laughed so hard she nearly fell off her rocking chair.

I realized: I'd never heard Anna laugh, not like that.

I had done that.

Inside, something was happening; someone was shouting. Someone yelled, "Find it!" We turned to look through the window.

Mrs. Taylor stood near the sink with her hand over her mouth. Anna and I looked at each other, rose, and stepped inside the house, abandoning our plates on the porch, though I did glance back at mine and hope that the bugs wouldn't find it before I returned.

Deirdre and Skylar were madly throwing our day packs off the pile. "It's the orange one," Deirdre said, and then I saw Ryan.

The plate of fried chicken had spilled at his feet. He grabbed at his neck, which was almost the width of his head. His eyes had caved in and his lips had shriveled. His mouth was open; he gasped for breath.

"FIND IT!" Cath yelled, terror in her eyes, in her frantic hands, as she kneeled next to Ryan, not sure where to touch him. Across the kitchen, Elliot slammed down the phone receiver.

"I—I just used regular vegetable oil," said Mrs. Taylor, pleading with Elliot, who rushed past her and helped Ryan down onto the linoleum floor.

Deirdre found the Epi-Pen in the side pocket of Ryan's pack, and she was the one who jammed it into Ryan's thigh. "Did it go?" she asked, voice breaking, and she looked inside the pen, unsure. She jammed it in again, though it only held one shot.

And we waited, hands over mouths.

I looked at Anna Verges: her lips were closed loosely and her eyes were glass. She was no longer there. Her arms dangled, limp. Anna Verges was gone.

Ryan found his breath, but it was shallow. He'd told us how it happened. But none of us believed it would ever happen to him, with all his paranoid self-protection.

"You don't have an allergic reaction the first time you eat something," he'd told us. "The first time, your body doesn't like it, and it builds up antibodies." The things designed to protect you were what killed you. They stopped the blood from flowing. They shut the organs down.

Ryan's blond hair spread out on the floor. Cath did chest compressions. Elliot looked out the window as the paramedics pulled up. He fled to meet them, and they banged in with a stretcher and syringes and activity.

My head was a wasps' nest, vibrating with sound. I looked over at Anna Verges and saw something die.

We slept at base camp that night, in a cabin with bunk beds. We fit in one large room. The springs sagged and the pillows were hard and flat like stacks of t-shirts. It was pure luxury. Ryan slept at the hospital. We were told that he was alive, but that was all we knew. "I'll give you an update when we have one," Cath said, and then disappeared to the mysterious place leaders slept when they were at base camp.

The unstated fact was that no one even liked Ryan. This only made us feel worse. We roasted our marshmallows without joy, not saying a word, listening to sugar burn and crackle.

It was something about human frailty that pierced us more than the idea of losing Ryan himself. But something hit Anna at a different vital weak spot. Veronica muttered clichés meant to make us all feel better and simultaneously broadcast her distress—"He'll be okay, he'll be okay, he has to be." Anna stared into space until it was time to return to our bunks, then rolled over to face the unfinished wood wall. I had claimed the bunk above her.

After sleeping outside for so long, it was odd to realize how much we could hear each other inside the cabin. Every crinkle of pack liner or rummage through a food bag echoed in the contained space. The sound of Anna's breath seemed amplified as if through a SCUBA mask. Then I realized she was crying. Anna Zec saw her too, and awkwardly giggled before turning to shove her clothes into her sleep sack.

The truth was I had been plotting my seduction from the second I discovered there was a chink in Anna's armor. I planned for it to be this night. I knew how it would go. I would go to her with my need, tell her I couldn't sleep, and ask her to come with me to the downstairs sitting room with its tattered easy chairs and cozy fireplace with no fire. I would need her, and she was most herself, she was her biggest, best self, when something was being asked of her.

I could still do it, and I knew it.

I climbed into bed with Anna and stroked her hair. Her body warmed the length of my body. I heard some whispers behind us, and wondered if the voice I heard was Skylar's.

Veronica and Anna Zec were elbowing each other over the one sink in the room when Cath returned with good news. "Ryan is going to be fine," she said. Her posture had returned to the rigid, leaderly uprightness we'd come to resent. Her smile was genuinely happy. "He'll be going home, but I thought you should know right away."

Anna cried harder for a minute, then stopped, took a deep sigh, and rolled over to face me.

Tears clung to her lashes as she blinked. I felt her breath on my mouth and the pads of her toes on the top of my foot. My clit felt like a ripe seed pod waiting for something to brush past it so it could flip inside-out. But we had come too close to losing something, and I couldn't make my move. I rubbed away Anna's tears with my thumb. "Tell me what's going on with you," I said, the way a leader would say it. The way a grown-up would say it. It was time to grow up.

ACKNOWLEDGMENTS

Thank you to the teachers who first read these stories, and the sketches that became these stories: Edwidge Danticat, E.L. Doctorow, Chuck Wachtel, Wayne Johnson, Maria Flook, Doug Bauer, Rick Moody, and Amy Hempel.

Thank you to the editors who first brought these stories into the world: Kelly Grey Carlisle at *Prairie Schooner*, Jill Adams at the *Barcelona Review*, Sven Birkerts and Eric Grunwald at *AGNI*, Hannah Tinti at *Washington Square*, and Ralph Pennel at *Midway Journal*.

For their professional support, I thank the New York University Creative Writing Program, the Bennington Writing Seminars, the Vermont Studio Center, Putney Student Travel, Emerson College, and Grub Street.

Thank you to Rachel Kushner for "action poems" and to my sister Amy Jones for "rexies." Thank you, Lisa Tozzi, kindred gringa spirit, for all the hours of coffee and *chisme*, and for some of the lines in "Heathens." Thank you to Dave McCrea and Karina Salguero for night drives around San José and for being my Costa Rican tether. I am grateful to Outward Bound, a far more responsible organization than Florida

Expeditions. Thank you to Kyle Minor for choosing these stories for the New American Fiction Prize, and to David Bowen, Okla Elliott and Raul Clement of New American Press for being champions of all that is right in the literary world.

"Sin Alley" is based in part on a series of interviews conducted by Jacobo Schifter and recorded with his analysis in the life-changing book *Lila's House: Male Prostitution in Latin America* (Haworth Press, 1998). I thank you, Mr. Schifter, for all your good work.

Thank you, thank you to my families: my parents, Susan and Rees Jones; my sister Amy Jones; my wife Kate Bonsignore; our children, Grayson and Cora Blue. And a very special thanks to all the young people I've worked with who have shared their stories. You courageous souls. Thank you is not enough.

photo credit: Aram Jibilian

ALDEN JONES's memoir, *The Blind Masseuse*, was longlisted for the PEN/Diamonstein-Spielvogel Award, winner of the Independent Publishers Book Award in Travel Essays, and a *Huffington Post* Best Book of 2013. Her stories and essays have appeared in *Prairie Schooner*, *AGNI*, *Post Road*, and the *Barcelona Review*, and have been anthologized in *Best American Travel Writing* and *Everywhere Stories: Short Fiction from a Small Planet*. She lives in Boston.

CPSIA information can be obtained at www.ICGtesting.com
Printed in the USA
BVOW05s2351080614

355720BV00002B/4/P